The Seventh Station

Also by
Ralph McInerny
The first
Father Dowling Mystery
HER DEATH
OF COLD

THE SEVENTH STATION

STATION

by
Ralph McInerny

A
FATHER DOWLING
Mystery

THE VANGUARD PRESS

For Charles Sheedy

The Seventh Station

1

WHEN ROGER DOWLING went on retreat in August, he had the sense of being driven from his rectory rather than of withdrawing from it for a short period of intense prayer.

"It'll do you a world of good," Marie Murkin, his housekeeper, assured him. Dowling's golf clubs were slung over her shoulder. He had the fleeting thought that Mrs. Murkin could turn a fairway into a Via Dolorosa if she ever got onto one toting that bag.

"I'm not taking those."

"You're not serious! Monsignor Hunniker lived for his annual retreat. Thirty-six holes every day. He came back brown as a berry and fit as a fiddle."

Dowling took the clubs from her. If his predecessor Hunniker was her standard of the good pastor, he would always fall short of it. Hunniker's weights were still in the basement, under the punching bag. Muscle-bound, skin tone good, the picture of health, Hunniker had been felled by a stroke at forty-two. So much for the wisdom of this world.

To escape from Mrs. Murkin, Dowling took the golf clubs into the study. A young priest looked up from the desk, his eyes widening in moral comment at the sight of the clubs.

"Got everything you need?" Dowling asked.

"Thank you, Father."

His name was Bovril and he was on loan to the parish while its pastor went on retreat. Bovril was in street clothes, clericals, high Roman collar; Dowling would have liked to approve of the young man. Not many priests still had the good sense to dress as priests. Unfortunately, Bovril suggested one possible reason for the reluctance of the many. His blueblack hair was shaped in a fluffy bell, his wide almond eyes looked unblinkingly through wire rims whose lenses were large enough to provide for several pairs of ordinary glasses; olive skin and a mustache at once full and silky drooped at the corners of his mouth. The fey young friar seemed costumed rather than dressed. Dowling, against his grain, resented Bovril's easy assumption of the pastoral desk.

"Doesn't the air conditioner in your room work?"

Bovril looked puzzled. His large liquid eyes turned to the humming air conditioner in the window as if he were noticing it for the first time. Without it, he would have melted in that suit.

"I thought I'd be more accessible down here."

"Ah."

Did Bovril have visions of broken souls streaming to the rectory door while he was in charge? Did he dream of ministering to them with his bookish spiritual counsel and sending them healthy away? The few vagrants who might show up would be dealt with by Mrs. Murkin. Bovril would have to content himself with the surer and sacramental help he could give in the confessional.

[2]

"I'm getting a ride to the retreat house so I'll be leaving my car here. You're welcome to use it." Dowling removed the key from the ring and put it on the desk.

"You're going to Assisi House?" Bovril's tone was a bit remote.

"Yes." It was a retreat house run by Bovril's confrères, the Franciscans. It was located on a lake fifteen miles west of Fox River in an area recently annexed by the city.

"Why Assisi House?" Bovril seemed to have decided on the direct approach.

"Why not?"

"I don't know if you made inquiries, Father." Bovril's eyes dropped to his manicured nails. "The truth is, Assisi House is not one of our more up-to-date places. I mean in terms of *aggiornamento,* of course. Father, there you will have difficulty believing that the Second Vatican Council ever took place."

"I see." The fact was that Dowling was counting on this. He had no desire to waste his time in encounter sessions or other excursions into amateur therapy. In his bag was the *Divine Comedy,* the Third Part of the *Summa,* and the *Dialogues* of St. Catherine of Siena. His was to be a private retreat, but he had made certain that he would not be surrounded by a psychological freak show parading as a new approach to the spiritual life. It was nice to have this corroborated by Bovril.

"Please don't think that that place is typical of our province."

"I'm sure it isn't."

"Have you read this?" Bovril lifted his book from the desk so Dowling could see its cover. *The Forgiveness of Zen.* On the back of the jacket a doughlike face smiled perfervidly at whom it might concern, a manic glint in the authorial eye.

[3]

"Not yet," Dowling said, suppressing a shudder. "I'm going to put these upstairs."

Slinging the strap over his shoulder, he headed for the stairs. The clink of his irons brought Marie from the kitchen.

"Lunch is nearly ready," she announced. "Is Mr. Keegan coming?"

"He'll be here."

"Why don't I put those on the porch, Father?"

His hand closed over the leather head-covers of his woods. With his elbow he brought the bag close to his body. "I'll be right down."

He fled up the stairs like an errant caddy and put the clubs in the closet of his room. He closed the door on them with almost a twinge of guilt. Marie Murkin made golfing seem a moral obligation.

He sat on the bed and put a match to his pipe. He had golfed hardly at all since being assigned to St. Hilary's parish in Fox River, Illinois, half a year ago. After all those years on the archdiocesan marriage court, stationed in Chicago, unaware of changing seasons, he marveled at the coming of spring and felt the lure of the golf course. As it turned out, he had preferred the quiet of the rectory, the undemanding round of pastoral duties, and his friendship with Phil Keegan, the spoiled priest who was chief of detectives in the Fox River Police Department. Phil had been at Mundelein, in the class behind his, though Dowling had no memory of Phil at the seminary. It was Keegan's pleasure, widower that he was, to look back on those seminary days with a heightened nostalgia. As a priest he would have made a good cop. Thank God that is what he had become.

Dowling waited in his room until he heard the doorbell ring and then the sound of Marie Murkin admitting Phil Keegan. It seemed safe to go down then. He found Keegan receiving a limp handshake from Bovril, who had been brought from the study by the sound of the bell. He seemed to be studying Keegan for signs of spiritual need.

"Mr. Keegan is a detective," Dowling told Bovril. "Chief of detectives."

"A cop?" Involuntarily Bovril took a step backward.

"You diocesan?" Keegan asked Bovril.

"Oh, no!" Bovril's eyes darted to Dowling as if exempting him from the implied condemnation of the secular clergy. "I am a Franciscan."

Keegan nodded and said nothing. Dowling knew what Keegan thought of the Franciscans.

"Lunch is ready," Marie announced.

They ate swiftly, at least Dowling and Keegan did. Bovril crumbled bread, toyed with his salad, took his knife to a single cold cut as if he were a scientist driven by nothing more immediate than the ends of pure research. He spoke of a Franciscan parish in Chicago to which he had been briefly assigned.

"That's a rough neighborhood," Keegan grunted. The detective, huge, hirsute, uncomfortable, refused to look at Dowling's ethereal replacement.

"The result of oppression. What we should be doing there is organizing, working for social justice, getting out into the streets." Bovril made this sound vaguely like going on safari. "This turned out to be a minority view. A minority of one." He smiled a martyr's smile. "Masses, confessions, one's whole day spent in the church, a vast sooty place just chockfull of simpering statuary and the smell of paraffin." He paused. "The men there are not unlike those at Assisi House."

"There is not much oppression in Saint Hilary's," Dowling assured him.

"Just what is the profile here, Father? Middle class?"

"I never gave it much thought."

"Any blacks or chicanos?"

"Only a few."

"Has any effort been made to bring more in?"

"How do you mean?"

"Well, maybe a parish housing committee, pledged to affirmative action. Often it is the realtors who are holding things back. And often the realtors are Catholics."

"I hope you don't plan any demographic experiments this week, Father."

Bovril smiled sweetly. "Things have a way of getting in motion wherever I am."

And so, finally, leaving was like an escape, although Dowling had a feeling of uneasiness about what Bovril might try to foment in the week of his absence. The young priest carried the pastor's bag out to Phil Keegan's car. Marie Murkin stood on the front steps. She seemed to be crying. Good Lord. He told Bovril to be patient with Mrs. Murkin.

"She'll be a big help to you if you let her."

"Don't worry, Father. I'll be fine."

"He'll be fine," Keegan repeated with a snort when he pulled away from the curb. "Where did you find him?"

"I didn't choose him, Phil. All I wanted was a priest to be there while I'm gone, to say Mass mainly. Just hold the fort."

"He's more likely to hand it over to the Indians."

Once out of the city, Keegan's manner changed. The country around Fox River had surprised Dowling at first, and it continued to surprise him. Now in August the fields seemed cornucopias, overflowing with the burden of their crops. He was fairly sure of corn and wheat, but beyond that he dared not go in identification. He asked Phil what a field they were passing contained.

"Beans. Soy beans."

Dowling felt free already. Concern for St. Hilary's slipped away as they drove.

"Why you making your retreat at this Franciscan place?"

"Do you have something against it?"

"I thought the archdiocese had regularly scheduled retreats for its priests."

"It does."

"Well?"

"Assisi House is convenient," Dowling said less than candidly.

"The priests there friends of yours?"

"No."

Keegan shook his head. "I don't get it. Why spend a week with a bunch of Franciscans you don't even know when you could be with your own, people you went to school with?"

But that of course was the point. Roger Dowling had no desire to spend a week playing cards, staying up too late, trading memories with men he had known all his life. In such circumstances making a retreat was too easily confused with the imaginative effort to get back to the days of one's youth, to remembered innocence. Keegan would love a week of that. He could never get enough of talking of the old days, of Quigley and Mundelein. Dowling had never asked Phil why he had left the seminary. He would bet that Phil had hated the place while he was in it and had been happy to leave.

"You should make a retreat, Phil."

"Yeah."

They fell silent. It occurred to Dowling that this was the first time he had presumed to give Phil Keegan spiritual advice. Phil was a good Catholic, a daily communicant, a conscientious and just policeman. And he was lonely, his wife dead, his children gone. His job was his life. No wonder memories appealed.

For Dowling himself, of course, a retreat was not simply desirable. As a priest he was expected to make an annual retreat, to withdraw for prayer and meditation and recharge the batteries on which his work as a priest depended. The archdiocesan retreats provided a minimal opportunity for that. Not that they weren't heavily organized. Three or four conferences every day, given by experienced retreat masters, often genuinely holy as well as eloquent men. But such retreats had the air of an alumni reunion. Besides, more frequently now, such gatherings were subjected to the innovative antics of a revolutionary retreat master. There had been ecumenical forays, conferences by Methodists and Lutherans. Dowling was more than happy to be going to Assisi House.

When Phil turned in at the gate and started up the blacktop road bordered by whitewashed rocks, the low brick building of the retreat house appeared against a backdrop of weeping willows.

"It even looks Franciscan," Phil said enigmatically.

"How do you mean?"

"I don't know. It just does. I can always tell these religious order places."

Dowling doubted that, but there seemed no reason to argue the point. Phil stopped at the entrance, under a porte-cochere, and declined Dowling's invitation to come in and see what it was like.

"I better be getting back. Well, have fun."

"Thanks for the lift."

"Give me a call when you want to come back."

He stood watching Phil drive back out to the road. It was like seeing a dock recede, getting under way. He picked up his bag and pulled open the door and stepped into what he was sure would be a week of peace.

So much for the wisdom of the other world.

2

INSIDE was a lobby reminiscent of a motel. Chairs and couches with plastic-covered cushions, several wire bookracks filled with edifying paperbacks. A fat man wearing shorts, a dress shirt, sunshade hat, and dark glasses was pensively turning a rack. It complained as he did so. Dowling went to the desk. Behind it a small white-haired priest in the robes of a Franciscan slept in a chair, his hands folded as if in prayer, his mouth open. Dowling was reluctant to disturb him. He put his bag on the floor and faced the lobby.

The fat man had taken a book from the rack and brought it to within inches of his dark glasses. He seemed to find the legend on its cover uninviting. He stuffed it back where he had found it. He had trouble doing so and several books fell to the floor with a loud slapping sound. The priest behind the counter came awake with a start. He looked at

Roger Dowling and this seemed to compound his momentary confusion.

"I'm Roger Dowling."

"Yes."

"I'm here to make a retreat."

"Oh yes, Father."

The priest got to his feet and came to the counter. He held out a gnarled hand. "I'm Father Pius. Your reservation is here somewhere."

Pius began to rummage in a drawer, talking to himself as he did so. Dowling found this incompetence reassuring. He handed Pius the letter he had received confirming his reservation. Pius took it as if it were a precious incunabulum. He hummed and nodded as he read it.

"It doesn't say what room you're assigned to, does it?"

"Are there many in residence this week?"

"Oh no. We're seldom busy any more." Pius smiled, revealing a gold-filled lower tooth. "We've been renewed nearly out of business." He laughed insouciantly. "But then we took the vow of poverty, didn't we? Let's see."

There was a plan of the house, first floor and second floor. It might have represented the decks of a liner. Again Dowling felt that he was setting out to sea in a ship of peace. There was a group of six from Fox River, perhaps Father Dowling knew them? To his relief, he did not. The names were the names of strangers. They were in the care of Father Placidus. Dowling was given a schedule of the group's day so he would know when the chapel was in use.

"Anyone else?"

"Just you, Father."

"Good."

"I see what you mean. Well, actually, there are lots of rooms. I suppose you'd like to be apart from the others?"

Dowling said he would and Pius pointed to a corner

square in the plan of the second floor. "Two-eleven. You'll like that. There are two windows, you see, because it is a corner room. A lovely view of the lake. I'll take you up."

"I think I can find it."

"It's no trouble."

Pius lifted a section of the counter and came into the lobby. The fat man by the bookrack had been following the exchange at the desk. He smiled and nodded at Father Pius.

"There are more books just outside the chapel, Mr.——"

"Connolly."

"And there is a small library in a corner of the rec room. This is Father Dowling. He is from Fox River too."

Dowling would have preferred not meeting anyone. He took Connolly's hand. He disliked sun glasses that concealed the eyes of the wearer.

"What parish you in?" Connolly asked.

"Saint Hilary's."

"Old Saint Hilary's," Connolly mused.

"Here on retreat?"

It was a stupid question. Pius stood beside them as if happy to have brought them together. Connolly nodded. From what Dowling could make out of Connolly's expression, the man seemed sheepish about his presence at Assisi House.

Finally Pius started off. Dowling followed with his bag. He had the sensation that Connolly was watching them climb the stairs to the second floor. An odd man. He seemed out of place here. Perhaps in another era Assisi House had received many like Connolly, but that era, as Pius had remarked, was over. There were not many left who saw the need for a spiritual retreat. He would not have thought of Connolly as one of those few. Of course this was unfair. He did not know Connolly. With luck he would not get to know him either. He meant to steer clear of the other retreatants while he was here.

The room Pius left him in was indeed nice. Bright

and clean, its two windows open, admitting a summer heat that seemed somehow muted by the nearness of the lake. He looked out and saw a path leading away from the house, winding through some willows and continuing toward the lake. He had only a glimpse of the water through the trees. There was no one in sight. Apart from Pius and Mr. Connolly he had seen no one. He stood in the center of the room. This is what he had wanted: solitude, quiet, a chance to be alone with his thoughts, alone with God. Now that he had it he felt unready. Perhaps he should take the tour of the house he had told Pius he did not want. Better to see exactly where he was before he became a recluse.

They had come up the stairs at the far end of the house, the south end where the lobby was, and then come down a long narrow hallway, past the closed doors of rooms not in use. The intervals between the doors had struck Dowling as small and he was relieved when Pius opened the door of 211. It was sizable. The advantage of the corner room. Stepping into the hallway now, he opened the door directly opposite his own to find the twin of the staircase on the south end. It brought him down into an area off which the chapel, the rec room, and the refectory opened. As Pius had said, there was another bookrack there. Voices came from the rec room and the distinctive crack of billiard ball meeting billiard ball. Dowling caught a glimpse of several men, no more like what he would have expected to see than Connolly had been. The smell of cigar smoke. He opened the chapel door and went inside.

It was empty except for a Franciscan in a back pew who turned and smiled at Dowling. Dowling was reminded of Bovril and thoughts of St. Hilary's flooded his mind, bringing back apprehension at what Bovril might stir up in his absence. He knelt and stared at the gaudy altar. Thoughts of divinity here seemed candied ones. He closed his eyes. My Lord and my

God. Christ present in that tabernacle. He prayed that his retreat would be a good one. When he opened his eyes he was startled to find the Franciscan standing beside him.

"I'm Blaise."

"Roger Dowling."

"This your first time at Assisi House, Father?"

"Yes."

"I thought so."

Blaise's habit had a tailored elegance and the cincture that hung about his waist was of an incredible whiteness. His sandals had brass studs. Blaise stepped back and Dowling had the absurd feeling that the Franciscan was modeling his habit. What would St. Francis have made of Blaise, Dowling thought unkindly. *Well, what would Christ make of me?*

"Have you been shown around?"

"No."

"Come." Blaise took his elbow and there seemed no charitable way to escape. Dowling, groaning within, allowed himself to be escorted from the chapel. Blaise waved in the direction of the rec room, identifying it, and swept on to a door that let them outside. They took the path to the lake. There were crucifixes at intervals, the Way of the Cross, fourteen in all, meditations on Calvary. The devotion was a special concern of the Franciscans. It would be good to make the stations, in the old phrase, but now, in the presence of Blaise, Dowling's thoughts were not disposed to meditation.

"Isn't it lovely?" Blaise cried with a proprietory air.

Dowling agreed that it was. Involuntarily he asked Blaise if he knew Bovril. Blaise himself was bald, his china-blue eyes were not aided by glasses, but he had the same air of bellicose naïveté that Dowling's replacement turned upon the world. Blaise thought a moment, then said that he did not know Bovril.

"He's in this province."

"Oh, no doubt." Blaise smiled. "Do you know all the clergy in the archdiocese of Chicago?"

"Of course not."

Blaise's smile seemed to say Q.E.D. The young man began to speak didactically of St. Francis then, a sketch of the saint's life, the spirit of the Order. "Actually disorder would be more accurate. It has split a dozen ways over the centuries, especially the nuns. Among the men there are blacks and browns, shod and unshod, bearded and clean shaven. That is as it should be. We are not an army, like the Jesuits. Even the Dominicans are better organized than we." Blaise smiled shyly. "One of my greatest devotions is to a Dominican."

"Catherine of Siena?" Dowling guessed.

"An even greater maverick." Blaise paused on the path, as if giving Dowling another guess. Dowling could see the lake now, not a large lake, its surface perfectly smooth in the August afternoon. "Savonarola," Blaise said.

Dowling looked at him with surprise. Blaise had dropped his coy manner. "A great man," Blaise said. "A misunderstood man. A martyr."

Dowling felt that he knew Blaise's type. A passionate seeker after the antic and offbeat. He had met devotees of Theresa Neumann like that, and people privy to private revelations, full of certainty as to the approaching end of the world. Dowling had no opinion on Theresa Neumann, a German stigmatic, and as for the end of the world, it seemed as likely to arrive today as any other time. What he could not understand was the relish with which the fanatic dwelt on the coming destruction. Thus Blaise on Savonarola, or so it seemed to Roger Dowling. He turned and looked back toward the house.

"I think I'll be getting back."

"You haven't seen the lake."

"Another time, Father."

The younger man seemed delighted to be addressed so

formally by his senior. He nodded, indicating that Dowling might go. And Dowling went, not swiftly, not lagging either. He was going to his room and stay there. Even at Assisi House, distraction awaited around every corner. Better to keep entirely to himself. Thank God for Pius. He had already decided that he would go to confession to the old priest, but if he had been unsure, Blaise would have settled it. Pius had the look of a man for whom sin was a serious matter and mercy more serious still. Savonarola. Dowling shook his head. Maybe the Florentine scourge was, as Blaise thought, an unacknowledged saint. And maybe he was a half-demented fanatic. There was evidence both ways. Perhaps there always is. But it was not a matter Roger Dowling had to decide, thank God.

After a nap, he read the *Summa* for an hour and a half. Someone had slipped another copy of the mimeographed schedule under his door while he slept. Supper was at 6:15. Almost he decided to skip the meal, but that was to invite a headache and a sleepless night. Besides, such dramatics might be misinterpreted as ascetic. But he waited until nearly 6:30 before going down. He filled a tray at the food line and took it to a table where Pius sat with another priest. This was Father Cyprian, the superior of the house. He was tall and thin with a gray crew cut, revealing long teeth when he smiled. At a large round table another priest, presumably Father Placidus, sat with his improbable group of retreatants. Blaise was nowhere in sight.

"You say a morning Mass?" Cyprian asked.

"I say a noon Mass in my parish. I would like to say a morning Mass here."

"Good enough. Placidus lets his bunch sleep late. They'll have a Mass this evening at eight. So the chapel is free in the morning. Pius says his at six and I follow. Say from six-thirty on you have the green light."

The food was institutional fare but Dowling, never a

gourmet, ate it without noticing. Except the bread. It was dark, almost black, grainy and good. Dowling assumed it was the *spécialité de la maison.*

"Only lately," Cyprian said. "For a month or so. A man came in off the road, a tramp, and wanted a handout. We get a lot of them, of course. In return, he offered to bake bread." Cyprian laughed. "Usually we have them help with the lawn, do a little yard work, that sort of thing. But this fellow wanted to bake bread."

"He needed special flour," Pius said.

"Flours. Mainly rye. We're hoping he stays a long time."

"I don't blame you. It's delicious."

When they had taken their trays back to the window, Cyprian leaned down and pointed into the kitchen. A man stood looking out the window, smoking a cigarette. "That's Waldo, our baker."

He looked like neither baker nor tramp nor any other particular thing to Dowling. Aware of the eyes on him, Waldo turned from the window. His expression was one of insolence. He dropped his cigarette to the floor and ground it under his heel.

Dowling went up to his room to find Connolly waiting for him in the hallway. He had taken off his sunvisor and was no longer wearing dark glasses. He had small eyes and thin hair, slicked down on his head.

"You wouldn't have a drink, would you, Father?"

"I'm sorry. I don't drink." He still said it as if it were a duty to reveal his inability to tolerate alcohol. "Isn't there something available downstairs?"

"Beer."

Despite his own past, Dowling could detect no telltale signs in Connolly, but of course it was silly to think there are universal traits of the alcoholic. And had he not himself long gone undetected by others? He had a sudden epiphany. That

[16]

must be the nature of Placidus's group, men drying out, looking for a spiritual motivation to quit. It made sense. It explained the unlikely look of Connolly and the others.

"I'm sorry."

"Well, I thought I'd ask."

Connolly shrugged and opened the stair door and was gone. Inside his room, Dowling had the sudden certainty that the few things he had brought with him had been tampered with. Connolly? Had he already looked for a bottle before asking Dowling if he had one? Perhaps he had gotten out of the room just in time and then stood waiting for Dowling to emerge from the staircase. The poor devil. Dowling knew what addiction to alcohol could do to one, and prowling about someone else's room was the least of it. His ring of keys lay on the dresser. He knew he had put them in his shaving bag, happy in the knowledge that he would not need them for a week. Why would Connolly be interested in his keys? Dowling turned the ring to see if they were all there, the key to the rectory, to the church. . . . The car key was missing. And then he remembered giving it to Bovril. Had the one key missing been the one Connolly had been in search of? Surely he must have come by car himself?

"By bus," Pius said. "A VW bus brought them from Fox River."

"I don't see it in the lot."

"It went away again. I suppose they met someplace in town and were driven out together. Saving gas, you know. Would you like a beer, Father?"

"I don't drink."

"Beer isn't drinking."

"For me it is."

Pius looked at him and seemed to understand.

"Is that the nature of the group Placidus is taking care of?"

[17]

"Drinkers? Oh. No. Now, Waldo is another story. No, they're all businessmen, I think. God knows they drink enough beer."

"How long have they been here?"

"Today's Sunday? They came yesterday."

"For how long?"

"I'm not sure. Placidus will know."

Dowling could see that the old priest did not approve of such curiosity. He did not approve of it himself. He was here to make a retreat. He had been here nearly half a day and there had been nothing but distractions. He wished Connolly had not come to his room. He wished his mind did not insist on concluding that Connolly had been looking for car keys. Surely if the man wanted to leave, all he had to do was leave, call a cab, call his family, call whomever had brought him in the VW bus. Dowling just did not think Connolly was desperate for a drink and would steal or borrow a car to go where he could get one.

"There's television in the rec room," Pius said.

"Thanks for the warning. No, I'm going to my room."

He had restored Pius's faith in his seriousness in being here. The old priest put a hand on his arm and Dowling felt that he should ask for a blessing. But he didn't. He started up the stairs, annoyed at his own pride. He was sure that a blessing from Father Pius would be a blessing indeed. When he reached the second floor, he remembered Blaise. He had wanted to ask about Blaise. Dear God in heaven, what a scattered soul he was. He walked down the long hall to his room, driving away all distracting thoughts. Behind his closed door, he pulled a chair to the window and sat. With the twilight twitter of birds and the scent of the lake bathing his senses, he read the *Summa* of Aquinas.

Some hours later he awoke with the birds. It was four o'clock. It could not have been much after nine when, unable to see the page of his book, unwilling to turn on the lights, he had gone to bed. A good night's rest and now in the morning a cleansed mind to be filled with thoughts of God. Washed and dressed, he stood at the window. To go down to the chapel now, to say Mass before Pius, would seem an affectation: a visiting amateur Trappist instructing these seasoned retreat masters with his arduous schedule. Below him along the path the crosses of the stations stood in the dewy grass of dawn—a fitting way to begin the first full day of his retreat.

The devotion to the Way of the Cross had gathered momentum over the past several centuries until in every church, in intervals along the walls of the nave, seven on each side, were pictured or engraved the major episodes in Christ's sorrowful passage from his condemnation by Pilate to Calvary and crucifixion and, finally, burial. The outdoor stations at Assisi House were sculptured on blocks of granite; a small cross rose from the top of each of them. Roger Dowling moved slowly along the path, stopping at each station, studying the sculptured episode—Christ condemned to death, Christ takes up his cross, Christ falls the first time beneath the cross, Christ meets his sorrowful mother. Dowling stayed a long time at this fourth station with thoughts of his own mother filling his heart and animating his devotion to the Queen of heaven and earth. Roger Dowling was Mediterranean in his devotion to Mary. A day without the recitation of the rosary would have been a dead day to him. The thought of any mother meeting her son in so dolorous a situation wrung the heart, but when the son was Jesus and the mother Mary, a vast new dimension was added to the mystery of such sorrow. Dowling remembered Lenten Fridays when every parish had prayed the stations, the priest and acolyte in the center aisle, pausing at each station, the whole congregation genuflecting with them, joining in the prayers and hymns. Like so many other devotions, this one had gone temporarily into eclipse while liturgists pursued their off-Broadway antics. Bah. He banished this bitter meandering. He was not here to review the deficiencies of others.

Roger Dowling continued along the path. The seventh station commemorates Christ's second fall. Dowling studied the depicted scene but his eyes were drawn from the station. Suddenly present and actual horror joined the imagined one of his meditations. My God! A body lay in the grass, heavy with terrible gravity, the handle of an ice pick emerging from the chest.

3

PHIL KEEGAN sat on the balcony of his apartment in Camelot Estates, a glass of tomato juice in his hand, looking down at the quacking ducks in the artificial lake below him. Those whose apartments overlooked the lake had the habit of pitching toast and other tidbits to the ducks of a morning. No doubt it seemed a convenient and functional way of clearing scraps from the table when one had breakfast on the balcony.

The duck as garbage can. The expectation was now bred into the ducks. Each morning at dawn they began to pass in quacking convoy along the shore waiting for their feeders to appear above. Keegan, who had never been guilty of feeding the ducks, had become a principal victim of their noisy reveille. It was his fetish to sleep with his apartment open to the night air, the air conditioning off, such breeze as there was off the artificial lake and, beyond, the Fox River, all the relief he required. To shut the doors of the balcony would have considerably muted the morning racket of the ducks but Keegan persisted in keeping them open and in being brought, cursing, into each day by their cacophonous demands.

Of course he half enjoyed being annoyed. He was a widower whose children had not chosen to remain in the Midwest, let alone in Fox River, Illinois. Two daughters. A son might have stayed in the neighborhood. He was a lonely man. Thank God he was a busy man as well. He loved his work, he did it well, it was not simply a job. In his youth he had thought of becoming a priest. He had decided against that, but he had retained the notion that one should seek a calling and not just a job. Not a very fashionable way to regard being a policeman nowadays, perhaps it never had been, but it was Keegan's way. He was the instrument of the law, the law was meant to protect and preserve society, society was necessary for the well-being of man. He could build such syllogisms endlessly, especially early in the morning like this, an indelible mark of the years he had spent in the seminary. In the Sermon on the Mount, in the Beatitudes, Christ commended those who hunger and thirst after justice. Keegan hungered and thirsted after justice.

And after his breakfast. Was it their just portion those ducks thought they were demanding? Keegan scowled. That was the parody of justice one met too often. What I am owed, what you must give me. That was only half of it. Rights and duties, not just rights. He went into his kitchen and took toast from his toaster. He had not heard it pop, the slices were cold. He disliked cold toast. He liked to butter it hot so that the spread melted into the toast. He did not like the lardy look of unmelted butter on his toast. He took the slices to the balcony and pitched them over the railing. There was a crescendo of triumphant quacking as the ducks converged on the toast. Keegan looked down at them with faint disgust. Dowling would be proud of him. Dowling would be on the side of the ducks.

Dowling. Not gone a day and already Keegan missed him. There would be no phone calls this week, no get-together before the rectory television to watch the Cubs lose in daylight. Keegan did not relish the prospect of the altered week. Maybe he should make a retreat himself, think things over, sort them out. Bah. What else did he do when he wasn't working but brood about his life? He made a cup of instant coffee and sipped it. Someone else must be feeding the ducks now; their noise was no longer directly outside. He turned to his ringing phone. The day was beginning.

The murder was unusual enough for him to stop Peanuts from going on to the domestic quarrels, bar brawls, break-ins, car thefts, and the rest of it.

"Where was the body found?"

After a moment's silence, Peanuts said, "I'd better spell it."

Peanuts spelled the victim's name too. It made one fear for society to think that its safety was in the hands of people like Peanuts while most of the world slept. But Peanuts was directly related to two councilmen, his father and his brother. The lack of mental sharpness was a family trait, but it was a stupidity, not to put too fine a point upon it, so complete it transmuted into innocence. It was impossible to look into the muscled countenances of Peanuts, his father, and his brother, and not trust them. This was a considerable asset to the politicians, though the benefits to the city were somewhat equivocal. Keegan feared that Peanuts would be pressed into politics if he were ever forced out of the police department. This night assignment was an experiment, part of a continuing quest to find a place for Peanuts where he would do the least harm.

"Where was the body found?" Peanuts's spelling had gotten lost in the quacking of ducks.

Peanuts tried to pronounce it this time, making the place sound like a male brothel.

"Spell it again."

The letters took a moment before they fused.

"Assisi House?" Keegan cried.

"That's what I said," Peanuts complained.

Keegan told Peanuts to return to Assisi House with his report, with everything he had. He would meet him there. Keegan slammed down the phone, finished his coffee, shut the door of his balcony, and hurried from the apartment. Retracing the route he had driven the day before with Dowling, his mind spent equal time on the irony that it should have been Peanuts who responded to the call from Assisi House and that the first thing that happened where Dowling had gone in search of peace and quiet was a murder. If it was a murder. He must not forget that he was dealing with Peanuts. He would have to see the body itself before he believed it completely. And that, if Peanuts could be believed, was now safely in the morgue.

4

FATHER PIUS sat at the little desk in the room that had been assigned to Mr. Connolly. He was looking at the notebook the man had been keeping, apparently thoughts stimulated by Placidus's conferences. To pry like this while a person was still alive would have been indefensible, but now that Connolly was dead it was another story. Pius had not been impressed by the police. They spoke of murder and then did not ask about the dead man's effects. For example, this notebook. Pius thought it possible that these scarcely legible entries were important. They raised another possibility, it seemed, and one more tragic than murder.

Pius closed his eyes and prayed for the soul of the dead man. Mr. Connolly. It seemed a terribly formal way to refer him to God's mercy. The full name was written in the inside cover of the notebook, a standard kind, they sold them downstairs for just the purpose for which Connolly, George Connolly, had used his, to make notes on the spiritual conferences, to write down thoughts on his life. So Pius prayed for the repose of the soul of George Connolly. Either way it was a horrible way to go.

Father Dowling had wakened him and together they had gone down the path to the seventh station where the body lay. Dreadful sight. Father Pius had seen many bodies in his lifetime, but for the most part after they had been prepared for burial. Mr. Connolly had not made a pretty picture. Lying on his back, grotesque in his short pants, his belly seemingly slung to one side of his body, and then that handle sticking from his chest. Pius had felt a sharp pain in his own chest at the sight. He had gasped and Dowling had taken his elbow.

"You're sure he's dead, Father Dowling?"

"He is dead. I gave him conditional absolution. We're going to have to call the police. I'm sorry. There'll be a bit of a commotion, at least for a time."

"The poor, poor man."

"Did you know him at all?"

"No." The admission seemed an admission of guilt. Had he missed an opportunity to provide some help to Mr. Connolly? Pius remembered that he had been standing in the lobby when Father Dowling arrived the day before. He had been using the telephone when Pius returned from showing Dowling to his room. Connolly had hung up and placed a dime on the counter. Pius told him there was a more convenient public phone at the other end of the building if he wished to make calls.

Had that been the extent of his acquaintance with the dead man? Pius searched his memory for some possible exchange in the refectory, perhaps a meeting outside chapel. Nothing. Of course it was silliness to want such images of oneself with a dead person, as if he had somehow taken part of Pius with him into the next world. Silly and superstitious.

Someone was calling his name. Cyprian. Pius put George Connolly's notebook into the pocket of his robe and hurried out of the room. Cyprian was the superior of the house but Pius had seldom heard such authority in his voice.

Cyprian was in the lobby with the odd little detective who had been here earlier and a large man whose frown lifted in deference to the fact that Pius was a priest and then descended again.

"You found the body, Father?"

"He—it—was by the seventh station." He looked to the other detective for corroboration; he had taken him right to where the body was.

"What time was this?"

"Quite early. Perhaps four-thirty, certainly not much later. Father Dowling had to knock on my door for some time in order to waken me."

"Father Dowling!"

"Yes. One of our retreatants. He had seen the body while he was making the stations. He wakened early. That's not unusual the first morning here."

"Where is Dowling?"

Pius looked at Cyprian. Cyprian said that he would get Father Dowling. Mr. Keegan spoke to the other detective.

"Why didn't you mention Dowling?"

"This is the first I heard of him."

Keegan turned to Pius. "You didn't mention Dowling when the police were here earlier, Father?"

"I suppose I didn't. What earthly difference does it make? He came upon the body and came immediately to me. The point was to call the police. Are you a Catholic, Lieutenant?"

The little detective seemed amused.

"Did I say something wrong?"

"He's a captain."

"I'm Catholic," Keegan said. "Why do you ask, Father?"

"Father Dowling gave the man conditional absolution. But he had no doubt that Mr. Connolly was dead. I saw no reason to mention that he had seen the body first."

"That's all right, Father," Captain Keegan said, but it was clear that he was displeased with his underling. Pius wished he could say something that would help the little detective, but he could not think of a thing.

"Would you gentlemen care for coffee?"

"Thank you. I'd also like a room where I can interview people, something a little more private." Keegan looked about the lobby. Pius did too. He could see what Keegan meant. There was Mr. Crispi on the stairway, half hidden, no doubt eavesdropping so he could go tell the others what was going on. My, but this was a dreadful thing to have happen with retreatants in the house.

Pius took Keegan and his assistant to an empty room on the first floor, just next to Cyprian's office, and left them there to await the return of the superior with Father Dowling. He assured Keegan that Cyprian could provide him with the names of all those currently in the house.

In the kitchen Brother Terrence was in a sulk. Pius had to fetch a pot himself and fill it at the coffee urn. Through the open serving window he could see Placidus's group in the refectory, Crispi among them. Five left, a glum group and who could blame them? This could be a sign to them, a *memento mori*. He might suggest that to Placidus as the topic for a conference. Wasn't this life, after all? One of our number snatched away and the rest of us left wondering when our own time would come? We know not the day nor the hour, Pius mused. The coffee overflowed the pot and ran onto his hand. Terrence cried out at the sound of splashing on his floor.

"I'm sorry, Brother. Just leave it. I'll come back and mop up."

"Oh, I'll do it, Father." Terrence had the look of one about to enter the Coliseum.

"Where's Waldo?"

"That's what I'd like to know."

"You've had no help with breakfast?"

"No."

"You should have told me."

"What is going on around here this morning, Father Pius?"

"Haven't you heard of the dead man?"

It was clear Terrence had not. He crossed himself and his chubby lips moved in prayer. "Was it a heart attack?"

"Brother, they say it was murder."

"Murder! Which one was he?" Terrence looked out at the group in the refectory to see if he could discover who was missing. But retreatants were seldom more than torsos to him, moving past the window with their trays. He had never really noticed the faces of Father Placidus's group before.

Pius left the cook to his necromantic curiosity and went away with the coffee for the police.

5

As LONG as Cyprian was in the room with them, Phil gave no indication that they were more than acquaintances, but as soon as the superior had stepped next door to get the list of names of the retreatants, Phil gave Roger Dowling a fish eye.

"Some retreat."

"Amen."

"Did you know this guy Connolly?"

"I talked with him. Last night after supper he was looking for a drink. Maybe seven, seven-fifteen. Who is he, do you know?"

"Just the name. He has a factory of some kind on the south side. Not a big place, but he was doing well, as far as I know."

"He didn't strike me as the kind of man you would normally find making a retreat."

"How do you mean?"

"I don't know." Dowling hesitated. He really did not know. It was not the fact that Connolly had been looking for a drink last night. A drink or two was not unknown even on clerical retreats. He did not feel he should mention his unfounded certainty that Connolly had been in his room looking for his car keys. Keegan had a justifiable contempt for intuitions of that sort. Dowling remembered Connolly in the lobby when he arrived yesterday. It was odd to think Phil had been just outside the building then, that close to a man about to be murdered, and now they sat discussing poor Connolly. The lost look of the man as he turned the squeaky bookracks in the lobby stayed in Dowling's mind. Connolly had seemed more than just ill at ease. He was out of his element and he knew it. What had prompted him to come to Assisi House?

"Have you received any report from the lab?"

"No . . ."

Cyprian came in with the list of names and Keegan asked if he could use a phone.

"Why don't you use my office, Mr. Keegan? There's a phone there and it is larger than this room. I don't know why Father Pius didn't put you there in the first place."

"If you're sure it's all right."

But Keegan was already on his feet. The three of them went next door where Phil got settled at the desk. He looked at the list Cyprian had given him. "Six men from Fox River."

"Five left," Dowling said, then wished he hadn't when he saw the alarmed look on Cyprian's face. For the first time he realized what an event of this kind might do to the house of which Cyprian was the superior. Making a retreat at the scene of a murder might not appeal to many and those who did find it appealing were unlikely to be good retreatants. He indicated to Cyprian that he was sorry.

"They all came together?" Keegan asked. Cyprian nodded. "Who made the arrangements?"

Cyprian thought. His eyes seemed to glaze. "I believe it was Mr. Connolly. Yes, it was Mr. Connolly."

"He was more or less in charge then?"

"I suppose you could say that."

"I want to talk with everyone on this list. I want to talk with everyone in the house. Peanuts!"

Cyprian jumped at Keegan's shout. Peanuts appeared in the doorway, then came inside. This office might be larger than the room they had just left, but with Peanuts added it was pretty well full. Luckily there was not much furniture. The desk at which Keegan sat, with a window at his back. A bookcase on top of which a painted statue of St. Francis stood, his plaster wrist supporting an unspecifiable bird. The chairs Dowling and Cyprian occupied completed the furnishings, unless one counted the crucifix on the wall, behind which a drying spear of palm pointed vaguely heavenward. Keegan was explaining slowly and patiently to Peanuts that he wanted to interview everyone in the house.

"How many you got on your staff, Father?"

"There is myself, Pius, Placidus, and Brother Terrence. We are down to a skeleton crew." He looked at Dowling as if for understanding.

"Who takes care of the grounds? You got any non-clerical help?"

"Oh, I do all the clerical work," Cyprian said.

Only Peanuts did not wince.

"Don't you have a man who bakes bread, Father?" Dowling asked.

"Waldo? Yes. He has been helping Brother Terrence."

"Waldo. Is that his last name?"

Cyprian did not know. Waldo was the only name he had given. And then there was Jensen who took care of the grounds. He had a truck farm up the road and lived there with his family. And that was it. Peanuts was sent to talk to

Waldo and Mr. Jensen. Keegan told Cyprian he would speak with the retreatants first.

"Stick around, Roger. Okay? I know you're on retreat but I can't help that. You found the body. You might just as well listen in on these interviews."

Dowling nodded, trying to dissimulate his pleasure. Did he so welcome distraction from his purpose for being here? But how could he hope to meditate with the puzzle of Connolly's dead body preying on his mind? The sooner this was unraveled, the better. Then he could get down to the business of his soul.

Keegan called them Connolly's friends and Dowling thought of them as Placidus's group, but it was impossible to think of the five men as in any way making up an intelligible unit. Jim Wolmer, the first to come in, was thirty. He wore his hair like a helmet, with bangs on his forehead and covering his ears. His wide belt and loafers were white patent leather. He had clear blue insincere eyes and he bit his nails. That was the image of him that remained: someone lunching on his fingernails while he listened to Keegan's questions. This was his first retreat. George Connolly had suggested it and it had seemed a good idea to Wolmer. No, he didn't know Connolly well. He had been in the club once or twice. The club? Wolmer was the proprietor of a bar in the business district of Fox River. The Fox Tail. Keegan seemed to know it. Last night after supper Wolmer had played euchre with Crispi, Browner, and Marston until the eleven-o'clock news and then had gone directly to bed.

"You sleep like a log here," he observed.

"When did you last see Connolly?"

Wolmer had started on a thumbnail. "I saw him at supper. I don't know if he was in the rec room or not."

"What kind of man was he?"

"Connolly? I really don't know."

"No idea at all?"

"How could I? I told you, I met him, I saw him, maybe twice."

"And yet when he suggested that you make a religious retreat with him, you jumped at the chance?"

"Why not? You tell him, Father. It's something Catholics do."

"I'm Catholic, Wolmer. I know about retreats. But if I was going to make a retreat, why would I go off with a bunch of strangers?"

Wolmer thought about it. His face brightened when he had the answer. "With friends, how could you think? Do you see what I mean? Strangers now, they're different. They don't get in the way of your thinking about your life."

Crispi was the owner-manager of a motel, a short, self-contained man, wearing an immaculate sport shirt and navy blue slacks. He was in his mid-fifties but his hair was still black. His expression would have been cold if it had not been for his eyes. They were sad eyes, wise with the wisdom of failure. Moral failure. Crispi seemed to be prosperous enough.

"You're right, Captain. It is odd. Here is something odder. I am fifty-seven years old." He paused as if he found his own age incredible. "I don't like to think of all the people I've known who died before reaching that age. To me, it seems young. Of course I know better. What do I have? Twenty years at most, ten, five, a week? A man begins to think of these things. So when Mr. Connolly suggested spending a few days here, I took it as a sign. Who has led a life he would want his mother to know about? Poor Mr. Connolly. When did it happen?"

"We're not sure yet. Tell me about last night."

Crispi mentioned the euchre foursome. Why did that game sound contrived, an alibi? It rang no truer than the explanations given of coming here at the suggestion of George Connolly.

Browner was in insurance and oozed the bogus unction this occupation requires. He seemed relieved to deny that he had ever sold George Connolly a policy. He had no idea what sort of insurance Connolly might have carried.

"Is that coffee?"

"It's not very warm. I guess we don't have a clean cup either."

"I'll get one," Dowling offered. Getting out of the room was like leaving the confessional for a breather. In the kitchen, he asked Brother Terrence for several cups.

"How are you keeping it hot?"

"We aren't."

"Let me bring you some fresh, Father."

"Where is your baker?"

"Gone. Fled. Not so much as a good-by."

"When did he leave?"

Terrence shrugged. "His bed looks slept in."

"Where does he sleep?"

"It's not much of a room. Back there."

"Show me."

Terrence took him around the pie ovens and down a little corridor: two doors opened off it, a lavatory and the room where Waldo slept.

"Look, Brother, would you take that coffee to the police? They are using Cyprian's office. I'll be right along. Tell Captain Keegan that."

When Terrence had gone away, Dowling looked first into the bathroom. A sink, a stool, a shower. Impersonal. Waldo's room did not give many more signs of having been occupied. The room was very small, half the size of those used by the retreatants, its dimensions hardly greater than the single bed, which was not made. If Waldo made his bed every morning that might prove he had slept here last night, but was the vagrant baker so fastidious? In the drawer of the little table beside the bed was a copy of an anti-Catholic tract. For the author of the pamphlet the Church of Rome was the equivalent of Antichrist. Curious. What sort of man was Waldo?

This is what Keegan was asking Brother Terrence when Dowling returned to the office. Browner lounged in the hall. If he was peeved at being bumped for the cook he seemed determined to conceal it from himself. Self-confidence would be everything in his line of work; the least sliver of doubt could be the beginning of the end. How many hours had he put in of servile waiting while his smile announced to the world that business was good? His face lit up at Dowling's approach.

"I'm missing a conference, Father." He glanced at his watch.

"I'll tell him to hurry."

Inside, Terrence was saying that Waldo had come early in June, maybe late in May. His offer to bake bread had been accepted, even though this had meant purchasing the ingredients.

"I never make bread," Terrence confessed. "Waldo is a wonder at it."

"Is he a Catholic, Brother?" Dowling asked.

Terrence seemed surprised at the question. Apparently it was one he had never put to himself.

"Did he attend Mass?"

"Nooo. No, he didn't. Of course I didn't keep tabs on him. He is an excellent baker, but he just came in off the road. We get quite a few vagrants. We feed them but we can't keep them here. He was different. Because of the bread."

"You never talked religion with him?"

"I don't think so."

"Tell me exactly what he looks like," Keegan said.

When he had the description and had let Terrence go, Keegan called downtown and relayed the description of

Waldo. "I want him picked up pronto. He's a vagrant. Lesser roads, the railway, that sort of thing, I suspect. He may have been traveling for . . ." Phil looked at his watch. It was just after ten. "Say four or five hours. Let me give you this number, Horvath. What are you working on? Peanuts is still on duty and I need him fresh and alert for his next shift." The sarcasm was gentle but Keegan avoided Dowling's eyes. "Take down these names and see what you can find out about them. You got the name of the dead man. Talk to his widow. Peanuts broke the news to her so God knows what was said. Then these five men."

Keegan read the names of the euchre players into the phone and added that of Leahy, the fifth man. When Browner came in again he got his cup of coffee but had little useful information to give in return. He knew Connolly from the Athletic Club. The truth was, he had thought this retreat might open a few doors. Get a man thinking of the fragility of life and you have a man in a mood to think insurance.

"Now let me get this straight," Marston said. "We have a murder here, am I right?"

"It looks that way, Mr. Marston," Keegan agreed.

"And you are investigating that murder. In short, this is an official inquiry."

"Do you practice criminal law?"

"No. Corporate. I am an expert in corporate tax law. My offices are in Fox River."

"Are you Mr. Connolly's lawyer?"

"No, I'm not."

"When did you come to know him?"

"Know him? I didn't know him. We were acquainted. I think Browner introduced us, at the Athletic Club."

"Was George Connolly an athletic man?" Dowling asked.

"May I ask who you are, Father?"

"Roger Dowling."

"I asked him to be here, Mr. Marston. Father Dowling found the body."

"I see. And when was that?"

"About four-thirty."

"Four-thirty! Good heavens."

"Were you awake?"

"I was. The food here, while wholesome, has an unfortunate effect on me. I suffer from colitis, gentlemen, an unsavory truth, but there you are. I was up much of the night."

"Did you see Mr. Connolly after supper last night?"

Marston considered the question with closed eyes, an index finger bisecting his pursed lips. His head began to move slowly in a negative way. "No. I am not sure that I saw him at supper, for that matter."

"You were at table together."

"You're right." Marston looked at Dowling. Clearly he already saw his answers as part of a legal proceeding. "But I have no recollection of seeing him after supper."

That left Leahy. He was sixty, florid, smoking a cigar and clearly relieved finally to get his turn. Of course he knew George Connolly. He had known him for years. Before Connolly went into business for himself, he and Leahy had been on the same sales force at Illinois Cog and Wheel. Leahy himself was now a manufacturer's representative and he no longer saw Connolly much in the line of business.

"Where do you see him?"

"In church."

"Ah. You're in the same parish?"

"Let's say we go to the same church. Saint Hilary's. Old Saint Hilary's in Fox River. I was raised in that parish. Call it sentimental, but no other church seems to be a real church as far as I'm concerned."

[37]

"Who's the pastor there?"

"When I was a boy it was Father Gorham, a saint of a man."

"He's dead, isn't he?"

"God rest his soul."

Keegan pressed on. "Isn't the present man's name Hunniker?"

Leahy's nod was distracted and could have been interpreted as agreement or impatience at having his memory of the saintly Father Gorham disturbed.

"Who killed Connolly, Mr. Leahy?"

The fat man lurched at the question. "Killed him?"

"He was stabbed in the chest with an ice pick."

"My God." There was no doubt of the genuineness of Leahy's horror.

"Mr. Leahy, you're the first one who admits having known Connolly. How did you happen to come here on retreat?"

"Stabbed with an ice pick. I can't believe it."

"Is this your first time at Assisi House, Mr. Leahy?"

"Yes. Yes, it is." But Leahy's mind was drifting away. "My God," he said again, shaking his head.

"Do you know his family?"

Leahy puffed up, about to lie, then deflated. "No. No, I don't. The fact is I hadn't seen George for years when he called and suggested we get together. That's why I'm here."

"You hadn't seen him in years?"

"No."

"Except at Saint Hilary's?"

"That was years ago too. I haven't been a good Catholic, Father," he said, addressing Dowling.

"Do you suppose he was rounding up lapsed Catholics and suggesting they make a retreat together?" Keegan asked.

"I don't know about the others," Leahy said.

[38]

Keegan let him go. When they were alone they had a cup of coffee together in silence.

"That was a waste of time," Keegan said finally. "Did any of them look like a murderer to you?"

"They are a strange group, certainly."

"The ice pick came from the kitchen here."

"How do you know?"

"Brother Terrence."

"Waldo?"

Keegan shrugged. A running man draws attention to himself. But what was the motive? God only knew. But Roger Dowling knew as well as Keegan did that the motive for murder need not sound convincing to anyone but the murderer. Was Waldo seething with hatred of the Catholic Church, had he settled here as a self-assigned spy, a judge, a scourge of the Lord? Whether or not Waldo had killed George Connolly, some distorted religious motive seemed to explain the corpse's being placed at the seventh station.

"Jesus falls the second time," Dowling murmured.

Keegan looked at him, puzzled.

"The seventh station. That's where I found him."

"Let's hope Horvath turns up something." Keegan stood. "Well, I guess I can leave you to your prayers for the time being. I'm going to have a talk with those two priests."

"I'll tell them you want to see them."

"Pius first. I may not see you again before I go."

"Good luck."

"Happy retreat."

They seemed to be trading taunts; in a mild way, of course.

6

Mrs. George Connolly, a silver-haired woman with that matronly look often vouchsafed in seeming consolation to the childless, had been unhinged by the news of her husband's violent death and was under heavy sedation in the care of the family physician, Dr. Simmons. Horvath was told that Mrs. Connolly would be incommunicado for at least twelve hours.

"She has never confronted anything like this before, Lieutenant," Simmons said. "How many of us have?"

"Did you know Connolly well?"

"In a medical sense."

"Not socially?"

"No." Simmons seemed mildly to insist on this. "He was not in good health. He drove himself too hard. I had warned him about that. Actually I had suggested a vacation. I wonder if he went on retreat in response to that advice?"

"Was he in the habit of making retreats?"

"Not that I know of. Of course there is no reason why I should know one way or the other." Simmons stroked his blonde mustache and looked out the window at the green expanse of the Connolly lawn. They were standing in the living room. "He might have mentioned it when I suggested that he should get away, but I don't remember the subject arising."

"Mrs. Connolly would know."

"No doubt. I've arranged for a nurse to stay with her. As soon as she arrives I must be going."

Horvath looked around the house, not quite perfunctorily. He did not believe this house would deliver up a clue. Mrs. Connolly was a better bet and Horvath resented the fact that Simmons had put her under before he had had a chance to talk to her. Cruel as it seemed, an hysterical widow is a more reliable source of information than would be the subdued woman who emerged from the sedative Simmons had administered. The mind, like the body, adjusts to shock; the habits and reticences of ordinary days begin to assert themselves again.

The den did not look like a place where anyone had worked or, for that matter, even relaxed. Like the rest of the house, it was too orderly, too much a setting to be admired rather than a place to dwell in. Horvath sat at the diminutive desk and pulled out one drawer after another. One of the Connollys was compulsively neat and he was certain it would be Mrs. Connolly. This home would be her castle. The contents of the desk drawers—stationery, stamps, Scotch tape, scissors, the instruction booklets for a host of appliances, household bills—suggested only an extremely well-run home. Better to move on to Connolly's office.

The front bell rang and Horvath heard Simmons admit a woman. The nurse. They passed the door of the den and went upstairs to where Mrs. Connolly lay in drugged unconsciousness. Horvath decided to go.

Connolly Tool and Die was a one-story cinderblock building in a neighborhood that seemed, in its fallen condition, to welcome such industrial invaders. Maybe a dozen cars in the parking lot. The office jutted out from one corner of the rectangular building, an addendum whose windows wore Venetian blinds and the reflection of the noontime sun. The receptionist was an attractive but not beautiful honey-blonde in her thirties. She looked up when Horvath came in but her fingers continued to move on the keys of her typewriter. The ID he showed her silenced the machine.

"Business as usual?" he asked.

"What else are we supposed to do? Is it really true? Has Mr. Connolly been murdered?"

"It looks like it."

Her name was Caroline Perth. She was a widow with one child, a son in the fourth grade, and she had worked for Mr. Connolly for a year. Ever since her husband died. Clearly she wondered what would become of her job and herself and her son now. Horvath had no answer to that.

"I called the house and a doctor answered."

"Mrs. Connolly is under sedation."

"I know it doesn't seem right, just going on. Do you know I am actually typing letters he dictated before he left?"

"When did he leave?"

"Saturday. He must have come in on Saturday morning and worked a few hours. He filled three belts with dictation."

"Anything unusual?"

"What do you mean?"

"I don't know. Is it any different from what he ordinarily dictated?"

She shook her head. She thought the world of Mr.

Connolly, and made no bones about it. She liked Mrs. Connolly too, not that she really knew her. She wanted to know how Connolly had died but before Horvath could tell her she held up a hand to stop him. She didn't want to know. Her eyes brimmed with tears. Horvath asked about the factory. Was Connolly doing well? Had there been anything unusual lately, any indication of apprehension or fear? Caroline Perth had not noticed anything. She asked Horvath if he thought she should make some sort of announcement in the shop. The foreman had been in and they had decided they knew too little. That is when they had decided to carry on as usual. Horvath had no advice for her. She was not happy about Horvath going into Connolly's office. She came along with him and hovered near. She was the kind of woman Horvath had never understood; they had several in the department. Transferring all that womanly devotion and concern to a job, putting more into it and deriving more from it than made any sense. Caroline was the typical devoted secretary, not likely to take kindly to a stranger's rummaging around in her boss's private office.

If Connolly had been in some kind of business difficulty, Horvath was not the man to discover it. As far as he could see, the office provided no hint that its occupant was in imminent danger of being killed. Horvath had the feeling he was wasting his time, but he stayed on anyway, not wishing to feel hustled on his way by Mrs. Perth. Finally she went back to the outer office, leaving the connecting door open, and in a few minutes the sound of typing began. What does happen to a small business when the owner dies? Horvath thought of the men in the shop, men whose plans had been based on the continuation of Connolly Tool and Die. Who could blame them, and Caroline Perth, if they took the boss's death as a personal blow?

When he came out of Connolly's office, he pulled the

door shut behind him. "Keep his office locked, Mrs. Perth. We'll have experts go over everything thoroughly. No one goes in there, okay?"

"Not even me?"

A shrug seemed the best answer. He was not about to tell a secretary how to do her job.

7

WHEN HE saw Horvath come out of the office, Jim Findley sat perfectly still. He had parked his car in the lot next to Connolly's and knew that Horvath was unlikely to notice him. One of the untouted advantages of the now standard headrests in automobiles is that every parked car looks occupied. Findley had slid down in his seat so that the headrest was higher than his head. He felt like the invisible man, or some malevolent spirit. It wasn't that he hated Horvath. What he hated was the goddam security the lieutenant represented and that Findley had cast away in the hope of making it big on the outside.

Findley was short and thin and large of nose, of comic mien despite the fiercely fostered self-image that had dictated his resignation from the department and had, against the tide of misfortune, sustained him for five years as a private investigator. Someone more candid with himself would have been able to admit the mistake, but Findley, who had never risen on the force above the routine of tooling around town in a squad car, had been undone by the rash of television serials devoted to private eyes. Like others in uniform, he had scoffed at the unrealism of such shows, had shaken his head in disbelief at the happy accident that enabled our hero to solve the case and make the police look like a bunch of dumb bunnies, but in his heart of hearts he did not doubt. If such shows collided with his own experience, what did he really know, a cop in the Fox River, Illinois, police department, not even a sergeant?

His first temptation had been the seamy side of the city revealed to him in the line of duty; there was a fascination in the yonder side of the law and there had been a stretch when, off duty, he had haunted the sleazy bars to which, on duty, he was called to quell disturbances. Two drunks battling over some broad. With his partners he had marveled at the depths to which man can fall—and secretly hankered to take a dive himself. It was during this period that Norah had left him. At the time he had been glad. All she thought about was his putting in twenty years, getting his pension, and then taking on another job. Then they would be on easy street. For that he was expected to expend twenty years of his life. After the divorce she had gone to the coast and married again. Without the thought of a wife to nag him about it, Findley found the honky-tonks less attractive. He didn't like to drink. He stayed home and watched TV and became hooked on the private eye shows.

James Findley, Private Investigator. That legend seemed to form upon the screen as he watched. He could easily imagine himself out of his rut, doing exciting things, commanding bulky fees, the envy of his erstwhile cohorts on the force. Soon he was in the grip of the idea, unable to free himself of it, unwilling to, suddenly certain that, knowing Fox River as he did, he could make a pile and be his own man besides. Was his resignation partly in belated defiance of Norah? That was another question he did not ask himself. He was like a kid walking dazed from the movie house, his head ahum with pictures of himself doing the deeds he had just admired on the silver screen.

So he made the move. Keegan told him he was nuts. Horvath advised against it. He thought that he detected the faintest signs of envy in both men. With his police background he was a shoo-in for the license. He rented an office, put an ad in the yellow pages, sent a photocopied letter to every lawyer listed in the Fox River directory, and waited. His savings oozed away. He tried for a loan and was refused. He was reduced to taking on security jobs in shopping centers, in parking lots, wearing a uniform again, the sort of thing cops did as moonlighting, but it was all he had. Just when he might have returned to the force, sadder but wiser, he had the bad luck of some good luck. A lawyer hired him. That first big check seemed to say he had turned a corner. There were other smaller checks to come, mostly from lawyers, but sometimes from a disgruntled husband or suspicious wife who was reluctant to pay off whether the news was good or bad. He learned to get as much money as he could in advance, and that was never enough. He moved to a smaller, cheaper office; finally he worked out of his apartment. What did he need an office for?

Somehow he had survived. From time to time he had thought of moving his operation to Chicago but his knowledge of the city was unsure. Go in with a large agency? Never. If he was going to work for somebody else, he would go back on the force. He was his own boss. That was the point of it. What is so bitter as a romantic dream gone sour? Watching Horvath cross the street to his car, Findley followed the lieutenant with hate in his eye, as if Horvath was the explanation of the dim performance of James Findley, Private Investigator.

Maybe it was only that he knew what regular cops thought of his ilk. It was what he himself thought. Unbothered by clients in his first office, he had checked the addresses of the two other private investigators listed in the book. One was Clementino, a retired detective who hadn't been all that good. A good address, but of course Clementino had his pension. The other turned out to be a local phone for a Chicago agency. Findley fairly lusted to know what business the others got and it seemed an ironic commentary on his pretensions that he was never able to find out.

When Horvath had turned a corner, Findley put his car in gear and drove out of the lot. He had had no trouble tailing Horvath from Connolly's house and he expected no trouble now. Good old Peanuts. Findley had a copy of the list of names Horvath was checking out; and he had taken the precaution of jotting down the addresses, too, before parking around the corner from Connolly's house and waiting for Horvath to arrive. Technically, of course, he was supposed to pass on what he knew to the police. That was what he would tell Gregory. And that is what he would do unless Gregory came across. Finally, after five long lean years, Lady Luck was smiling on James Findley, private eye.

8

THAT FIRST full day, Monday, at Assisi House, Roger Dowling did not say his Mass until noon and this contributed to his feeling that he might just as well have stayed home for all the time he was able to devote to putting himself in the presence of God and taking stock of his life. What a morning. Kneeling in the chapel, making his thanksgiving after Mass, he could hear the murmur of voices from the refectory. He had made a commemoration of George Connolly in his Mass, praying for the repose of the poor man's soul.

Our fear of death is more often of natural death, of cancer and heart attacks, some betrayal of the body. Except of course when we fly. Dowling at take-off always breathed a prayer from the breviary. *In manus tuas, Domine, commendo spiritum meum:* "Into Thy hands, O Lord, I commend my spirit." Taken from the Church's night prayer, it seemed appropriate to what could in seconds be the violent evening of one's life. And then the plane would soar upward and onward safely and one grew used to the assault on nature that flying is. Our sense of mortality does not involve the fear that we will be murdered, stabbed with an ice pick. Yet George Connolly had been. Why?

If anything could prevent Roger Dowling from making a worthy retreat it would be that unanswered question. Would he be able to drive it far enough from his mind to render it harmless? It would be nice to think so, but he knew himself well enough to doubt it. He lowered his face into his hands. Had the body of George Connolly been put in his path for some purpose? Was he wrong to regard this event as an intrusion, a distraction? Nothing happened without a purpose. He firmly believed that. Why then had he been the one to discover Connolly's body? Perhaps it was self-indulgent to wish that he could put aside thoughts of the murder and dwell on the condition of his soul. He looked up at the tabernacle. The trouble with prayer was that one formulated one's own Delphic answer to petitions and then professed to be hearing the voice of God. What he could do for Connolly was to pray for the repose of his soul. And of course he must pray for the murderer too.

Connolly's murderer. Merely a phrase. Whom did it describe? Keegan had not ruled out the men in Placidus's group, not really. Nor would he find it difficult to imagine one of them driving that ice pick into Connolly's chest. Keegan could probably imagine Pius doing it. And he would be right. We are all capable of the worst. Not out of the blue, perhaps; one must decay gradually before the truly heinous deed becomes a possibility, but that gradual decay is all but invisible to others. It is to avoid those first seemingly innocent downward steps that we must pray, that we must make retreats. Yes, it was conceivable that someone as outwardly pious as Pius should have, over the years, become a hollow man, impervious to his surroundings, guilty of a hundred small betrayals of his vocation until, finally, seemingly suddenly but as the predictable fruit of his past life, he plunged that ice pick into George Connolly.

But why? If Pius was not logically impossible as a suspect, who could rule out Crispi, Leahy, Browner, Wolmer, or Marston as plausible suspects? But again there was need of a motive; and Phil Keegan was confronted with the less than credible fact that none of the others had really known Connolly although in some way he was the reason they were here and here together. So Waldo, the vagrant baker of delicious bread, the man who had worked in the kitchen from which the ice pick had come, and who had disappeared when the corpse appeared, was the ranking suspect. The question of motive could be faced later. Roger Dowling hoped it had nothing to do with the tract he had seen in the drawer of the table beside the unmade bed in Waldo's diminutive room. What a cell of a place that was. A man could sit there, lie there, seethe with a generalized hatred of the world, driven perhaps by a deranged prejudice, then strike out impersonally at Connolly as somehow the vehicle of all that Waldo could not abide.

Roger Dowling shook his head. Less probable things turned out to be true every day. Waldo was one more to pray for.

The sounds from the refectory increased. Lunch was ending. Dowling felt suddenly hungry. The door of the chapel opened and Placidus came in. Faced into the chapel, he held the door open behind him for a moment, perhaps hoping to entice some of his charges inside for a postprandial prayer. No one followed him in. Dowling got up, genuflected, and went out.

Crispi and Browner were talking in the doorway of

the rec room but when they saw Dowling they stopped and turned away. The others were already busy around the billiard table. The serving window in the refectory was still open. When Dowling bent down to look in, hoping to signal Brother Terrence, Waldo stared back at him.

He stood there, as surly as Dowling remembered him from the day before, wearing a less than clean apron, guiding racks of dirty dishes into the washer. The noise of the machine was proportionate to its size. Dowling was certain that Waldo could not hear him if he spoke, so he went into the kitchen.

Terrence sat on a stool slicing vegetables into a pan held in his ample lap. He looked up with a smile.

"He's back," Dowling said in a low voice.

"Beg pardon?"

"Waldo." Dowling glanced in the direction of the washer.

"Yes. He's back. Somewhat the worse for wear, but he's back." Terrence spoke in a loud voice, clearly meaning that Waldo should hear him. Dowling turned to see Waldo looking at them oddly. Without changing expression, he raised his fist and beat penitentially on his aproned chest. Terrence laughed merrily. Dowling went over to Waldo.

"Could I speak with you?"

"Go ahead."

"Let's get away from this machine." The dishes sounded as if they were being broken into a thousand pieces in the entrails of the washer. Dowling went to the back of the kitchen and Waldo followed somewhat reluctantly.

"Have you heard of the man who was killed last night?"

Waldo nodded. "He told me." He was Brother Terrence.

"He was stabbed with an ice pick."

Waldo was impassive.

[51]

"Where did you go, Waldo?"

"You think I have to tell you where I go? I can **walk** out of here right now and never come back. No one has any claim on me."

"Do you know the police are looking for you?"

Waldo was genuinely surprised. "I don't believe you."

"Think about it. A man is found dead, stabbed with an ice pick from this kitchen. Someone who works in the kitchen is gone. . . ."

"I was drunk!"

"Tell me about it, Waldo. I can help you. The detective who is on this case is a friend of mine."

Waldo was a reluctant narrator, but he was frightened now. Perhaps he had had occasion to learn to fear police. His story had the ring of truth if not of plausibility. One of the men had come to him, wanting a car. Of course Waldo did not have a car. Wasn't there a car belonging to the house? Could Waldo get him the key to that? He offered twenty dollars for the key. Waldo was working for food and lodgings and the chance for some cash was attractive. It had been a long time since he had had a drink. So he fished the key from behind the desk in the lobby and gave it to the man. What man? Waldo's description matched Connolly. He had watched Connolly drive away. What time was this? Maybe eight o'clock last night. And then Waldo had gone in quest of drink.

"When did you get back?"

"Ask him." Meaning Brother Terrence. Waldo thought it had been an hour ago.

"Where did you sleep?"

"Don't you believe me?"

Dowling looked into the man's seamed face. No doubt Waldo had slept in many improbable places in his time. The man's scowl was a mask behind which moral weakness hid. His eyes suggested that he had long since stopped trusting or believing in himself. Dowling would have liked to know the long route Waldo had taken to arrive finally at his temporary abode in Assisi House. Where had the man gone wrong? But Dowling believed him. He told Waldo so.

"The police won't."

Of course he was right. Even if his story were ninety per cent true, it allowed for his return and the killing of Connolly.

"Are you a Catholic, Waldo?"

"I'm nothing."

"No beliefs?"

He snorted. Dowling might have just asked his opinion of Santa Claus. "What should I do?"

"Nothing. Go on with your work."

"What about the police?"

"I'll talk to them when the time comes. You don't have to go looking for them."

That was not the sort of advice Phil Keegan would appreciate, but the hunted look that had come into Waldo's face moved Dowling deeply.

In his room he settled down with Dante. He had brought with him a single-volume paperback edition of the *Commedia* he had picked up in Rome, in a bookstall near the Piazza Esedra. Not the best text in the world and the notes were elementary, but it was a convenient volume. It was also a souvenir of a pleasant visit to the Eternal City. He felt like hell this afternoon and turned to Canto XII, the seventh circle, the circle of the violent. By the banks of the Phlegethon.

There was a tap on the door and Pius looked in. "Are you busy, Father?"

"Come in, come in." Dowling put down his book.

Pius shut the door and stood beside it, apologetic, his hands hidden in the sleeves of his habit. "I am sorry your retreat has gotten off to a bad start, Father. Believe me, things are usually quiet as a grave here." The simile displeased him. He shook his head impatiently. "You were with Captain Keegan when he spoke to our other guests?"

"Please sit down, Father."

Dowling himself sat in the easy chair he had pulled to the window. The Way of the Cross, what he could see of it, brought back unpleasant memories of his morning discovery. Whatever bucolic aspect the stations took on in this setting, they were a commemoration of violence. Again he thought of the seventh station, Jesus falls the second time. Pius drew out the desk chair and sat on its edge, his sandaled feet emerging from beneath his robe.

"Are you bound by any promise of confidence about those interviews?"

Dowling hesitated. "No."

"Do they have any idea who did it?"

Outside the window, a catbird, elusive among the willows, was mimicking his betters. "Waldo's disappearance seemed suspicious to them."

"Waldo!"

"But he's come back. Apparently he was off on a drink spree. I advised him to sit tight. The police will make it difficult for him, but he denies having killed Connolly."

"Do you believe him?"

"Yes."

"Thank God. Father, did the police ever consider that this might not be murder at all?"

Pius had leaned forward. Clearly this was his reason for coming.

"You talked to the police yourself, didn't you?"

"I answered Captain Keegan's questions, yes. This is a terrible dilemma. I can hardly wish that it was murder, but I almost do."

"Why do you doubt it was murder?"

"It would be so much easier on his family, and on his good name, if he were thought to be a victim of murder."

"Instead of a suicide?"

"Yes."

Pius drew a notebook from his sleeve. "This was in his room, on his desk. The first time the police were here they did not even go into the room. When I saw what he had written here, well, I took it. I suppose that was wrong. But was it? My conscience does not guide me clearly on the matter."

Dowling took the notebook Pius held out to him. Keegan would hit the ceiling when he heard of this, first because Peanuts had overlooked it, second because Pius had taken it from the room. It would not matter whether or not the notebook was important. Flipping through it, Dowling had his doubts. Only half a dozen pages had any writing on them and they were not crowded. "The last things, heaven, hell, death. . . ." Dowling looked up.

"Notes on Father Placidus's conferences?"

"I believe so," Pius said.

"I don't find any indication of intent to commit suicide here." He did not want to tell Pius that Connolly had borrowed the house car last night. Where had he gone?

"Do you have a car here, Father?"

"You want to take that to Captain Keegan?"

"Oh, no. No. I just wondered if there is a car."

Pius came to the window and looked out at the lot, pressing the side of his face against the screen to do so. "That blue sedan is ours." Dowling, standing beside him, saw the car he meant.

"Is that the only one?"

"Jensen has a small truck, but he keeps that at his farm. Is this important, Father?"

"Not at all." And then he saw that Pius meant the notebook.

"Read the last page. That is why I took the notebook."

Dowling found the page and read: *Don't wait for the blow to be delivered. Strike first.*

"It could mean anything, Father. Just about anything but suicide. Have you ever had a suicide here?"

"No, thank God. But we never had a murder before either. Think of where he was found, Father. Jesus falls. Could the poor fellow have sought forgiveness for his deed by performing it there?"

Dowling wondered if Pius had more to go on than this notebook. These entries simply did not justify the fear that Connolly had killed himself. It seemed wise not to press the old priest. It could so easily be something that had passed between priest and penitent and it would be cruel to Pius even to intimate that he was disclosing a confessional secret by professing to find a suicide threat in Connolly's notebook. Returning to the opening pages, Dowling saw something he had not noticed before. Between two scrawled entries, neatly printed, was the name *Dolores.*

Pius went to the door. "If it is murder, I hope they don't catch the murderer. Is that wrong?"

"What you really mean is that you hope God catches him. But that may hinge on the police getting him first. Did Keegan talk to all the Franciscans here?"

"Yes."

"When I was in the office you didn't mention Blaise."

"Blaise?" Pius had his hand on the knob. He looked quizzically at Dowling.

"Yes. A young man. I saw him in chapel last night."

"I don't know any Father Blaise."

"He's a Franciscan. He wore the habit. He clearly belonged here."

"There is no Blaise here, Father Dowling. So far as I know there is no one of that name in the province."

9

Out of habit Keegan went to the noon Mass at St. Hilary's. It was always a safe haven when Dowling was the celebrant. Bovril was different in that Bovril was exactly what Keegan would have found in most of the parishes in town, in the state, in the country and, for all he knew, in the world. The time would come when a man would have to journey far to find a Mass celebrated with some semblance of the ancient reverence and with some hint that the point of it was to worship God.

Bovril, wearing only an alb and stole, his movements fluid and sinuous, grinned out at the sparse congregation, as if they were here to share a manic high with him. The regular clientele, ranging from middle-aged to old, was seasoned by one young mother whose two kids were already negotiating the back of the pew as if it were the start of an obstacle course lying between them and the street door. Keegan sympathized with them. He gritted his teeth, clamped his eyes closed, and concentrated on his rosary. Not even Bovril could prevent this from being a Mass, unless of course he forgot to read the canon. Bovril had a trilling tenor voice and turned everything into *a capella* song. For Keegan it was a penitential rite and he was glad when it was over and he could flee to his car. What was this week going to be like for Marie Murkin?

Later, in his office, he sat at his desk and reviewed where they were in the matter of the violent death of George Connolly. Murder one? Maybe not. That ice pick could have found its mark in a fit of passion, unpremeditated. In any case, it was murder. The lab report was in and the time of death had been put at between midnight and two in the morning. Peanuts's description of the condition and location of the body was a study in ineptitude. Keegan had looked around the seventh station himself. The flattened grass was greasy with the blood of the victim. So put the death from two to four hours before Dowling came upon the body. The corpse was identified, and origin of the murder weapon was known. There were no prints on it but Peanuts's. The dummy.

No word yet on the vagrant baker, Waldo, and Keegan did not like that. If they didn't pick him up right away, the chances were they would miss him altogether. The man's description suggested someone who had spent a lifetime eluding pursuers. But the fact that he hadn't been picked up was encouraging too. An innocent Waldo would have set out openly and been found in an hour. That he had not been suggested a furtive leavetaking. Cold comfort this. Keegan dreaded adding one more folder to the files of unsolved and thus unprosecuted crimes. There were too many such files now.

Keegan was uncomfortable with the idea that the system of justice caught in its net only a sample of the crimes being committed, though he knew this was probably the case.

But it was one thing to speculate about undetected, unreported murders, of murderers walking the streets unsuspected; it was quite another thing to have the corpus delicti, to have invested hundreds of man hours in an investigation, and then draw a blank. That was untidy, of course, and it was wrong. It was an indictment of himself and of the work he did. He did not want to believe that the penalty for known crimes involved an irrational lottery: some got caught and some did not. Keegan wanted them all caught. He meant to catch them all. Discouraging as the slim folder on George Connolly now was, he intended to get the man who had killed Connolly and see him stand trial for what he had done.

Dowling liked to contrast justice and mercy. Of course he was a priest and that altered his outlook, as it should, but Keegan was not sure of the contrast. Who was he to say that mercy and forgiveness did not come more surely to the criminal caught and convicted rather than to one who went unpunished? Wouldn't the one who got away revel in his luck, think he was one helluva guy rather than thank God he had not been called to account for what he had done? It was not that he might repeat what he had done; that was a matter that always obscured the issue. Did punishment prevent the repetition of the deed? If murder is wrong, one murder is enough. Keegan felt no obligation to prove that a murderer will repeat, his crime become a habit, as if it were the accumulation of corpses that was the problem. The single body of George Connolly involved guilt enough to send somebody away for life.

But who if not Waldo? Keegan almost dreaded being stuck with Waldo. It would be difficult having him judged on this case alone. Doubtless the man would have a record as long as your arm, minor offenses, time done here and there about the country, just the sort of defendant a jury liked. What did society have to lose by putting him away again, perhaps for good? Keegan's interviews at Assisi House had been unsatisfying. He agreed with Dowling that those five were unlikely candidates to be making a retreat. And together. How could there be no connection among them? Were any two of them strangers to one another? There was at least a link to a third man, to Connolly, yet the only one who had been willing to say he knew the dead man beyond mere acquaintance was Leahy and he was a liar. The only thing that made sense was that the five of them were there because Connolly had asked them to be. Perhaps he had forced them to be there, by some sort of blackmail. Or would it be *white*mail in this instance, Connolly intent on weaning them from their evil ways? Why had they not left Assisi House now that Connolly was dead?

Keegan picked up the phone and told the girl on the switchboard to get him Assisi House.

"Any special sissy, Captain?"

"Funny." He spelled it for her. Damned women, you had to hire them now, naturally. They were bad enough at jobs like the switchboard, but of course they all wanted to go out in prowl cars, quell riots, chase bank robbers, get in the way.

The girl mumbled away in his ear while she flipped through the directory. Keegan had a pencil ready to take down the number. He wouldn't go through this again.

"Here it is," she cried in triumph.

"I thought it might be. Give me the number."

She did. Then she rang it for him. The phone rang and rang. Keegan let it ring. Eventually the phone was picked up but seconds went by before anything was said. The voice was thin and birdlike.

"Father Pius?"

"Yes, it is." Pius seemed to think it cunning of Keegan to have found him there at Assisi House.

"This is Captain Keegan. I was there this morning."

"I know."

"Does Father Dowling have a phone in his room? I'd like to speak to him."

"Nooo. There's a pay phone at his end of the building, but it's on the first floor. There is no guarantee that anyone would answer if I gave you that number."

"Could you call him to this phone then?"

"All right. It might take awhile. I'll have to go up to his room and he'll have to come back here. Could I have him call you?"

"I understand the problem, Father. No, I'll wait."

He heard the phone being put down on a surface. It would be in the lobby or perhaps in Cyprian's office. Keegan tried to construct from the sounds that reached him an image of the place, perhaps even to discern the atmosphere of a retreat. The idea of withdrawing like that from the real world made Keegan uneasy. God knows he had sympathized with the five men he had interviewed. It was like getting caught in a brothel, the seeming public assertion of virtue that being at Assisi House was: each in his own way had conveyed to Keegan that he must not think the worst of him for being on retreat; he was only doing it to please a friend, as a favor to Connolly. Again the odd thought that Connolly had blackmailed the others into spending five days with the Franciscans came to Keegan. Imagine sitting around chatting with Father Pius. Not that the man wasn't a saint, but that said it all, really. What are you going to talk about with a saint? Little angels, special devotions, what heaven will be like? Keegan's faith was blind. He accepted it all. But the truth was he preferred not to talk about it.

"Roger Dowling. Is that you, Phil?"

"Sorry about calling."

"Has anything come up?"

"No. Question: Are those five I talked with this morning still there?"

"As far as I know. I'm certain four of them are."

"What are they doing there, Roger?"

"You know what they're doing. They're on retreat."

"Come on. You were there when I interviewed them. You were surprised yourself. Did you maybe get the idea that somebody had their number and the price was five days at Assisi House?"

Dowling's laugh was no help. Keegan waited for him to finish. "Phil, it's really not that bad. You should try it sometime."

"I mean like blackmail."

He sketched for Dowling the thoughts that had been running through his head. Out loud they sounded more far-fetched than they had as mere thoughts. At least Dowling agreed that Connolly seemed the only link among the five on retreat.

"So now, with him gone, they should hit the road?"

"That's the idea."

"They don't have cars. Remember, they all came together by bus."

"And you figure they're going to wait right there until a bus comes by to pick them up again?"

"Does Connolly own such a bus, Phil?"

"I'm still waiting to hear from Horvath. The time of death was between midnight and two. And we haven't picked up Waldo yet."

"About Waldo, Phil. He's back."

"What do you mean, he's back?"

"Back working in the kitchen."

"Why the hell didn't you call me? Doesn't he know we're looking for him?"

"I talked with him, Phil. He went off on a toot last night. Connolly gave him twenty dollars to filch the key to the house car."

"Roger, keep an eye on him. I'm coming right out

[62]

there." He slammed down the phone. Jesus Christ, he said, uncharacteristically. He tried to think of it as a semi-prayer. What was wrong with Roger Dowling? That place must be rotting his brain.

10

WALDO was a reluctant narrator but, with Phil Keegan acting prompter and Roger Dowling the audience, the baker's story emerged. The three men stood in the kitchen, a gleaming, echoing place redolent of many meals. Dowling felt ignored by Keegan but then he agreed with Phil's unstated but palpable estimate of his behavior, though he could not regret having tried to spare Waldo. But now Waldo's resentment seemed directed at him, perhaps explaining in part his hazy account.

"Now wait a minute," Phil said. "It's after supper, right? And you're standing where?" Keegan opened his arms wide, as if inviting Waldo to choose a place.

"I was doing pots and pans."

"Pots and pans. Good." Keegan marched them to the sink. "Then what? Mr. Connolly came into the kitchen?"

"I don't know his name."

"His name was Connolly. The shorts, the shirt, it couldn't be anyone else. When did you realize he was in the kitchen?"

"He came back here to the sink."

"Isn't that odd? Are guests supposed to be walking around in the kitchen?"

"I don't make the rules. I just work here. You think I'm going to throw him out or something? Maybe he's a priest, for all I know."

"He came up to you while you're washing pots and pans at the sink. What did he say?"

"He wanted to borrow a car."

"His words. What did he say?"

Waldo got the idea. "He said, 'You work here, don't you?' There I am with my arms in dishwater and he asks me if I work here. I just looked at him. He said, 'I need a car.' What can I say? 'I want to borrow a car. You got one?' I shook my head. So he says, 'There's got to be a car here.' I told him there was a car in the parking lot outside. The house car. Did I have a key? I said no. That's when he got out his wallet. You know, letting me see he's loaded. 'I want to use that car,' he said. 'Get the key for me.'"

"So you got it for him. Where was the key?"

"Behind the desk in the lobby."

"Come on." Keegan had Waldo by the elbow. "Is this the way you went?" Keegan was pointing to the door that led into the refectory.

"No. There's a short cut."

And so there was. A door that admitted them into the first-floor corridor at about midpoint. It might have been the door of a resident room as seen from the corridor. It locked behind them when it closed.

"Did Connolly go with you for the key?"

"Sure. He was anxious, I can tell you that."

They came into the lobby and Waldo stopped. Father Pius was behind the counter. The old priest seemed startled to see them. They must look and sound like strolling players.

Keegan said to Waldo, "Where were the keys?"

"What keys?" Pius asked.

"The car keys."

Pius pulled open a drawer and began to rummage about in it. His frown deepened. "That's strange."

"They're not there, Father?"

"It doesn't look like it. Sometimes they're hard to find "

"You gave Connolly the keys where? Right here? Where was he standing?"

"I was where Father Pius is. He was there." Waldo indicated a spot directly opposite. "I gave him the keys and out he went."

"The front door?"

"The front door. He wanted me to take him to the car, but if he couldn't find it, that was his problem."

"And you had your twenty dollars."

"That's right," Waldo said belligerently. "I went out the door right after him. I figured it was time I took a breather."

"We'll get back to that. Did you see Connolly driving the car?"

"While I was going out to the road, I heard the car start. In the parking lot. And then he came barreling out of there. He damned near ran me down."

They went outside to the parking lot. The keys were still in the car. Keegan took them and, inside again, made a phone call. He was impounding the car. Dowling knew that Phil expected that car to tell its own tale, to indicate where Connolly had driven and why.

"It was nice of him to bring it back," Pius said. Keegan had to give the old priest some of the story in order to explain why the car would be picked up.

"If it was Connolly who brought it back," Dowling mused. Keegan wheeled on him.

"*Now* you're curious about the car."

"Phil, I'm sorry. I was concerned about Waldo. You believe him, don't you?"

"I'm not done with Waldo yet." He turned to the baker. "We're going to retrace the route you took with your twenty dollars."

Waldo looked pleadingly at Dowling but Keegan hustled him out to his car. Dowling did not fear that Keegan would be rough with Waldo but it was a pathetic sight to see the vagrant go off in the police car. How often had hope died in him in similar circumstances, when he had fallen into the hands of the law with no veneer of respectability to protect him?

"What's going on, Father?"

It was Marston. The lawyer seemed more dressed up than he had previously; he now wore a colorful sport jacket over his dark shirt.

"More police routine."

"Who was that Captain Keegan took with him?"

"You haven't met Waldo?"

"Not one of the priests, is he?"

"He works in the kitchen."

"Would you like to go for a walk, Father?"

There were few things Dowling wanted to do less, but Marston's expression suggested that the request was not casual. Perhaps he was addressing him as a priest. Dowling nodded.

Marston said, "I find that the path leading to the lake offers the best itinerary."

Marston must have been in his mid-forties, but he was trim and hale, of very erect carriage, and Dowling had the belated fear that it was vigorous exercise and not a stroll the lawyer had in mind. Dowling stopped to light his pipe, hoping this would introduce a note of leisure. Marston watched him get the pipe going satisfactorily.

"Still smoking, are you, Father?"

"You quit?"

"I read the surgeon general's report from cover to cover. When I had finished, I gathered up every cigarette in the house and threw them in the trash. I haven't smoked since. Nor have my wife and daughter."

"Cold turkey?"

"When I balanced whatever small pleasure I derived from smoking against the statistical likelihood that I would die of lung cancer, stopping presented no problem whatsoever. The emphasis now is on heart-related ailments. That simply tips the balance further. It is not unlike the conferences Father Placidus has been giving us. For the first time I am seeing religion in terms of a balance sheet that truly makes sense to me. On the one hand, there is this life. Consider it from the most optimistic standpoint, imagine that you will live to be one hundred. I waive all consideration of whether so long a life would indeed be a blessing. Select the ideal maximum age. Very well. Within that span imagine whatever illicit pleasures and satisfactions you wish. Do not stint. Let them be many, various, and undiluted. That is the one side. But what is there on the other? An eternal penalty. Damnation. Hell. It is a bad bargain, Father. Worse than a bad bargain. To live as one should live is simply enlightened self-interest. Now, when one considers that the pursuit of illicit pleasure is almost never as I described it earlier, but is instead accompanied by every kind of inconvenience and unhappy consequence, an infinitely bad bargain becomes infinitely worse. The worst of both worlds." Marston nodded with satisfaction over these calculations. "This retreat has been a very profitable time for me."

"Then you're glad you came?"

"Absolutely."

They were now on the path that led past the stations. Those memorials to Christ's passion did not catch Marston's eye. His complete attention was on the cost accounting he had just described. Dowling wondered how he could convey to Marston that he had grasped everything except what truly matters in his new-found version of the faith.

"Have you ever heard of Pascal's gamble, Mr. Marston?"

"No, I haven't. Who is Pascal?"

"He was a seventeenth-century mathematician who was also a great religious writer. It was his ambition to compose a solid and unanswerable defense of religion. He wrote a great many notes for the projected work and they are what has come down to us under the title, *Thoughts* or *Pensées.*"

"I see. And what was his gamble?"

"It is a famous passage, but I am not convinced that it best conveys the spirit of Pascal. In any case, what you were saying reminded me of it. It goes something like this. Imagine that we have no way of knowing whether a life beyond this one awaits us. Of course the Christian religion is nonsense if there is no future life. Therefore, one might think, until he knows if heaven or hell awaits him, until he knows there is a future life, he has no solid reason for accepting Christianity. Pascal proposed that one gamble that Christianity is true, that one live his life on the assumption that there will be either eternal reward or eternal punishment. It is a gamble one cannot lose. Either Christianity is true, there is an eternal life and one's conduct earns him heaven, or there is no eternal life and one does not survive to regret his gamble."

[68]

"Wonderful!" There was a glint in Marston's eye. "What I was saying is more or less the reverse side of that gamble. I would like to read Pascal."

They had reached the seventh station. Dowling stopped. Marston stopped too. The lawyer was obviously enjoying this conversation. Dowling did not much care for himself in a didactic mood, but he was not through.

"As I said, I'm not sure the gamble passage is a good sample. Some critics find it scandalous."

"I can't imagine why."

"They feel it leaves too much out."

"If it encompasses time and eternity, there isn't much else."

"I suppose it's the motive they wonder about. It's rather difficult, on the basis of the gamble, to get much of a notion of eternal happiness."

"The fulfillment of one's every desire," Marston said with catechetical precision.

"The love of God." Dowling prevented himself from suggesting that the *of* was both an objective and possessive genitive. Dear God, how easy it is to prattle about such things. And he had come to Assisi House in order to stop prattling for a time.

"They find it selfish?" Marston asked helpfully.

"I think you're right."

"That seems somewhat carping to me."

"Perhaps. This is where I came upon the body of Mr. Connolly." He pointed and Marston turned to look at the spot. Dowling himself looked toward the parking lot. He could imagine a direct line connecting the parked and now impounded car and this seventh station.

Marston spoke. "When I asked you to walk with me, there was something I wished to say, Father."

Dowling nodded, his eyes remaining on the car.

"You were there this morning when I spoke with Captain Keegan. I was less than frank with him. Of course I chose my words well, there was no overt untruth, but I was not fully candid. To be sure, I had no obligation to be. It was not a court of law. Nonetheless, I am an officer of the court and I do not like to be at all secretive where an official investigation is concerned."

"I suppose it's not always easy to know what is relevant and what is not."

"This is relevant. Do you see that car in the lot? Connolly went off in it last night. I saw him from the window of my room."

"Weren't you playing euchre?"

"I was. I was also indisposed. You may remember that I mentioned suffering from colitis. I had absented myself from the game and gone to my room in order to take some Kaopectate. While I was there—incidentally, my window is that one, six from the far corner, first floor. You can see that I have a very good view of the parking lot. I heard someone outside. I turned off my bathroom light, I had not switched on the room light, and went to the window. I saw George Connolly get into that car and drive away. I will have to tell Captain Keegan this. And he will have every right to be angry with me."

"Actually, you're in luck, Mr. Marston. He already knows about the car."

"You're sure of that?"

"Positive."

Marston took a step back, releasing a sigh. "Thank God. As you say, I'm in luck. I would not want Captain Keegan to distrust me."

"Did you by any chance hear Connolly return?"

"No. I was up at approximately four-thirty, as I told Captain Keegan. If I understand the timetable, Connolly was already dead then. Indeed, the body had already been discovered."

"And of course the car was back where it belonged. It is in the same place it was when Connolly took it?"

Marston had to rise to tiptoe to get a better look and Dowling could see that he was not sure.

"Why don't we go over there? We can cut across."

Marston cast a fastidious glance at the intervening area. Bordering the path on that side was a strip of grass but beyond it lay an untended uneven field, whose rise between the path and the parking lot had caused Marston to stand on his toes to look at the car. Dowling started through the field, on a direct line, assuming that Marston would follow. Once into the field, he forgot the lawyer, his attention absorbed by what seemed to be signs of an earlier passage through the field. Connolly last night? Dowling altered his course so that he walked beside the apparent trail rather than over it and turned to warn Marston to do the same. But the lawyer was not behind him. He was on the path leading back toward the house.

"I'll meet you in the lot," Marston called.

Dowling continued toward the car but his eyes were on the ground to the right of where he walked. Those were definitely signs of a passage. Had this been Connolly's dolorous way, destined to end at the seventh station? Jesus falls the second time. The unerring straightness of the trail from car to station did not diminish the likelihood that it had been an intended destination, containing perhaps the meaning or explanation of Connolly's murder.

Dowling stopped. The weeds seemed trampled as if some scuffle had gone on. Was it only imagination that led him to see a terrible struggle going on here in the dark, only a few yards from the house? For he was certain now there had been more than one person in this field. But this was absurd. He was not Tonto. He had never been a Boy Scout. Who was he to pretend he could read the ground like a book? But Keegan had to take a look at this.

"What were you looking at?"

"I'm afraid I'm just a city boy, Mr. Marston. The wildlife one sees in the country fascinates me."

"It seemed the better part of valor for me to go round. That field may well contain pollinous weeds and I am allergic."

"Is the car in the same place it was in when Connolly took it?"

"I'm not positive. Certainly in the same part of the lot. Why is the car still here if Keegan knows about it? It represents valuable evidence."

"A van is coming for it."

Marston nodded in approval. "I had hoped we might go on to the lake." He looked at his watch. "But I must not be late for Father Placidus's next conference. Thank you for relieving my mind, Father. And thank you for drawing my attention to Pascal. How is the name spelled?"

Dowling spelled it for him, feeling like a pedant. Marston repeated the spelling, consigning the name, Dowling was sure, to a steel-trap memory, then turned and walked quickly back to the house.

Dowling looked back the way he had come, across the field to the cross on the seventh station, where two walks destined to end in death had intersected. Christ had risen and gone on after that second fall, but George Connolly, a fat figure in shorts, out of shape, out of his element, somehow the cause of five improbable men going on retreat, bade good-by to life at a memorial to Christ's own saving exit. Dowling prayed that that at least was not coincidence, meaningless, a jest of chance. May he rest in peace.

His thoughts turned suddenly to Blaise, the young man in chapel whom Pius did not know. Unnerving religiosity, the obscenity of his Franciscan habit cut from the richest cloth, turning him into a travesty of the Poverello. In the

Paradiso, where Dante places St. Francis, he laments the decadence into which his followers had fallen, their first fervor gone, replaced by the pursuit of favor and fortune, a compromise with this world. Was it unfair to see Blaise as the nadir of an ideal gone wrong? But why would Pius say he did not know him?

11

KEEGAN sat in Dowling's room, the notebook before him on the desk, finding it difficult to conceal his anger with his old friend. This evidence, added to the failure to let him know what Waldo had told him, was a terrible strain on the affection and respect he felt for Roger.

"Is there anything else?"

"Yes. Pius says that he doesn't know the Franciscan who called himself Blaise."

"Maybe you got the name wrong."

"Blaise is what he called himself. He was wearing a

Franciscan habit. I can't imagine that he could wander around a place like this unnoticed if he doesn't belong here. Pius says there isn't a Franciscan named Blaise in the whole province."

"Would that mean the whole state?"

"More than likely the whole Midwest."

"Who else was out there trampling up the field with you?" Keegan passed a huge hand over his face.

"You'll find the field in exactly the same condition I did, Phil. I was quite careful not to disturb it."

Keegan picked up the notebook and dropped it on the desk. The sound was a comment.

"This whole investigation has been a farce from the beginning. I'd like to blame Peanuts. I'd like to blame you. I blame myself. Do you know that I have not yet talked to the wife of the deceased? And I haven't got a report on the other five men from Horvath? At this rate, the statute of limitations will run out before I have anything for the prosecutor."

"I thought there wasn't a statute of limitations on murder."

"That's what I mean. Do you know where I went wrong? I didn't want to disturb the peace and quiet here. I didn't want to ruin your retreat. I still don't want to, but now I am going to do my job as I should have in the first place. We are going to comb the house and grounds as we normally would. We are going to have statements from everyone. We are going to run this investigation by the book and we are going to find out who killed George Connolly. I am going to set up shop right here. I am going to sleep here. I am not going to budge from this house until I have solved this goddam murder. Excuse me," he added perfunctorily.

"You'll like the bread."

"They remembered Waldo down the road at the joint he got to. He was there until closing time and he bought a bottle, a pint, when they threw him out. We found the place where he finished that and then passed out."

"I think you should find Blaise."

"Who's the head honcho of the province?"

"Cyprian will be able to tell you. Or Pius."

"You want to see about that, Roger?" He turned. "What's that?"

"The supper bell."

Dowling was as surprised as Keegan at the hour. They went down together and sat at a table apart from the others. Placidus ate with Cyprian and Pius, the five retreatants alone at their table. The refectory was a silent place. Everyone seemed to sense that the investigation had taken a serious turn.

"Your replacement is a choreographer, Roger."

"What do you mean?"

Keegan described the antics at the noon Mass and Dowling winced. He could not say he was surprised. But if he had needed any further proof that his annual retreat was ill-starred, Keegan's description of Bovril at the altar of St. Hilary's sufficed.

"Poor Mrs. Murkin. I must telephone and give her encouragement."

Keegan had beer with his meal and Dowling felt a faint twinge of his old fatal thirst. His rejection of Marston's computer version of the Christian life stemmed from the manner in which he himself had overcome the drinking that had brought him low during his days on the archdiocesan marriage court. It would be ludicrous to explain his stopping in terms of will power, some inner athletic trick, or as the logical consequence of the sort of balancing act Marston had described. He had come to see in his broken self what he truly was without God's help and it was grace that had enabled him to rise. To take pride or even satisfaction in the change would have been a denial of what had really happened. Now, sensing a vestigial thirst at the sight of Keegan's sweating bottle of beer, he realized how quickly he could sink again if all that stood between him and the abyss was his self-produced moral fiber. He and Waldo were more akin than the wary vagrant guessed, or perhaps would believe.

Keegan pushed back from the table. "Horvath should be here by now. I'll be in the office."

"Perhaps I'll look in later. I've yet to see the lake."

"There's a lake?"

"It's at the end of the path, out back."

"Where the body was found?"

"Yes."

They rose. At the other tables there seemed to be a determined resolve to act natural, with the usual unnatural result. Dowling felt that it was a kindness to the others to get Keegan out of the refectory. When they reached the hall, the sound of voices began behind them.

"I thought they kept silent at meals," Keegan said.

"It's not a rule."

Keegan continued down the hall to Cyprian's office and Dowling let himself out of the building. Where the stations ended, the path began a rather swift descent to the lake. There was a dock jutting out from the shore. Dowling walked out to the end of it and looked over the water in which the evening sky repeated itself. Assisi House owned the complete littoral of the lake and everywhere he looked he saw uninhabited shoreline. Whatever the ultimate fate of the retreat house, the Franciscans had a fortune in real estate here. Of course if they began to sell land, speedboats were sure to come and ruin with their roar the contemplative calm of the lake.

Had George Connolly ever been on this dock, had he ever looked out over this water? The vast mystery of death overwhelmed Dowling's mind. Time, perception, thought, involvement in and experience of the world—could all that simply cease, be reduced back into a lump of decomposing matter, the whole history of a life rendered meaningless by its total snuffing out? Pascal's gamble. For the first time Dowling felt the tug of the argument. It was not the best argument. It had the flaws he had hinted of to Marston. But perhaps there are moments when it has its uses, its force. Certainly the plea to plunge into this life as if it were all requires a constant turning away from the awe and dread and wonder that we feel at the fact of death.

12

Fox River, Illinois, originally a lovely little town west of Chicago, had been a victim of the westward movement that sent expressways, tollways, and interstate highways, together with land developers, into the blighted sunset. The huge sprawl of Chicago, itself somehow cleansed by its proximity to the lake, having nowhere east to go, went where it could, and dozens of independent communities had been cannibalized before Fox River felt the first signs of impending doom. The inexorable external threat had combined with the ethos of the day and, in the grips of a suicidal mania, Fox River succumbed to the carpet bombing called urban renewal. Its doomed downtown, already superseded by the suburban shopping centers, asphalt and steel growths around which jerry-built housing swarmed, multiplying as the metropolitan cancer went into metastasis, now delivered to the wrecking ball every building possessing even a minimum of style and distinction until the inner city seemed a mad mimicry of the threatening suburbs. Parking lots took the place of leveled buildings. Portage Avenue, once a thriving place of commerce, became a mall lined by empty shops and peopled by deracinated mendicant youths with an odd look in their eye and strange chemicals roaring in their blood while debris blew over the brick walks and collected in the desultory fountains. The town took on the look of the defeated side in a war that had never been openly declared.

Out of this, unlikely, a lean whistle in the dark, rose the upended rectangular box of the First Prairie Bank of Fox River, twelve sparsely occupied stories. The bank itself occupied the first floor, sharing it with a bookstore that specialized in greeting cards, and the Fox Tail, a bar that opened for business luncheons, thrived at the cocktail hour, and persisted until two in the morning as a nightclub of sorts. Lieutenant Horvath sat at its bar, a beer before him, methodically reviewing what he had learned.

If the Assisi House seemed an odd locale for that assembly of retreatants, the First Prairie Bank Building provided another. The Fox Tail was the bar Jim Wolmer owned. Marston had his offices on the seventh floor. The two top floors were a motel, parking provided in the underground garage, a special bank of express elevators whisking patrons past the intervening floors. Crispi was the owner of the motel. Three out of five, not bad, whatever it meant. Probably nothing. They already knew the men were from Fox River, that they were at least acquainted with one another. Small wonder then that they should be occupants of the same building, three of them, anyway. Horvath sipped his beer. Findley was in a booth behind him and he could keep an eye on him in the mirror behind the bar.

Findley had been with him all day, from the time he left the Connollys'. Horvath looked at his watch. Keegan was expecting him at that retreat house. But first Horvath wanted to sort out his thoughts and settle with Findley. Then he would go out to Assisi House. Keegan relied on him to lay things out as clearly as possible. He had thought of stopping at home to do this but talking to Lilian on the phone, or trying to, with the kids raising hell in the background, settled that. Lilian was a cop's wife. She didn't like it but she had quit complaining.

The bartender slid a Reuben sandwich in front of Horvath. "Anything else?"

Horvath drained his glass and pushed it across the bar for a refill. Findley wasn't eating.

Horvath had detoured to the john when he entered the Fox Tail, and when he came out and made his phone call he saw he had given Findley his chance to get in and settled in a booth. Did the sonofabitch really think he was undetected? The way it looked, Findley might be the best thing that had happened all day. What after all had he found out?

Mrs. Connolly, a blank, nothing at all. Nothing in the house either, at least on his preliminary look. The plant? Caroline Perth. Connolly's loyal secretary, widowed, young kid. Anything going on there? She could do a whole lot better than Connolly any day of the week. But what did better mean? Women aren't all that gone on looks. This was a truth

Horvath had learned from personal experience. It was still a source of surprise to him that Lilian had married him. She was the only girl he had ever gone with. In school he had been a jock, he had taken training seriously, it had been a welcome excuse for not having dates. He was convinced that girls found him ugly. He had been a monster man on the football team and that is what the guys called him, the monster man. A name like that affects its bearer. He felt like a monster. He could not say that Lilian was different from other girls, because he had no one to compare her with. He had met her when her little brother got into trouble. A long story. They got along. No sweat. But he had been surprised when she agreed to marry him. He couldn't even remember how he had asked her. After he was married, other women seemed to treat him differently, or was it that now he could recognize the symptoms? Not that he played around. He saw too much the results of that sort of crap, even if he had been inclined. Idiots like Findley. So Caroline Perth and Connolly were not an impossible combination. He could be King Kong and it wouldn't matter if he was kind to her. And there would have been the promised security of money. Of course there was the complication of Mrs. Connolly. The little Horvath had seen of her told him that Mrs. Connolly was a lady, regal. Even the blow of her husband's death had not taken that from her.

He dismissed the thought of hanky-panky between Connolly and his secretary. It was too speculative. But the thought did not quite go away. Small wonder. With something like that, there would be a beginning, a hook to start hanging things on. Not that he could imagine Caroline Perth sneaking out to Assisi House and putting an ice pick into her boss. Still, she had seen Horvath as a man. He had sensed it while they talked. Perhaps it was only an instinct. A woman, left alone with a child, needed a man to take care of her. Whether voluntarily or not, Caroline Perth's antennae would be out.

Unless the audit of Connolly's books turned up something, Horvath did not know where they stood. He wasn't really worried. With a thing like this, you nose around, do the routine, pursue a plan, but nine times out of ten something you hadn't dreamed of turned up and was the key to the whole mess. Patient persistence. He had learned that from Keegan. It worked, even when it shouldn't.

Marston's office had exuded prosperity. He had two partners, but he was Mister Big. Horvath had talked with the prosecutor and Marston was described as tops in his specialty, tax law. He was president of the county bar association, respected, regular, rich. His wife worked two mornings a week at the children's hospital, was a volunteer with St. Vincent de Paul, president of the local ballroom dancing club. One daughter, married, gone. The Marstons still lived in a house that must have been too large when their daughter was at home. Riches, rectitude, right living too, if working out in the gym of the athletic club meant anything. Marston was perhaps the only one of the five whose presence at Assisi House was not a complete surprise.

"Where's Wolmer," Horvath asked the bartender.

"You know the boss?"

Horvath fished out his credentials. No point in playing it cute. "Is he in?"

"He's out of town for the week. Chicago, I think."

"Where do you get in touch with him?"

"Me? I don't."

"The place burns down and you just wait for the boss to come home?"

"I guess Jerry knows where he is."

"Jerry?"

The bartender indicated a door to his right. Horvath took his sandwich and beer with him. There was a black and red coat of arms mounted on a wooden shield and attached to the door. "Wolmer" written in Gothic script. The bartender knocked and poked his head inside. When he reappeared he indicated that Horvath could go in.

Jerry was tipped back in the chair behind the desk, feet up, working at his nails with a letter opener. A miniature Japanese TV on the desk brought the Cubs afternoon game to his critical eye.

"What can I do for you?"

"He tell you who I am?"

"I know who you are."

"Where's Wolmer?"

"Unless it's an emergency, forget it. He'd kill me if I called him up for anything routine." Jerry did not look worried. He was fifty and fat and pale with the pallor of a man who has worked all his life in bars.

"But you could reach him?"

Jerry nodded. "So what's it about?"

"Just routine."

"Then I can't help you."

"How long will he be gone?"

"Today's Monday? He's due back Thursday or early Friday."

"What's the secret?"

"He just wanted to get completely away, completely out from under. I don't blame him."

"The place doesn't look all that busy."

"You wouldn't believe the aggravation." Jerry took his feet off the desk and turned down the sound of the set. "Years ago I used to dream of owning my own place. Work for yourself, be your own boss? Forget it. I started watching the guys I worked for. If that's independence, you can have it. When I'm through, I leave and forget it. The boss can never really leave and forget."

"They make more money."

"I'm not so sure. But say they do, what good is it? I

told you, they can't get away. Like doctors. What's the good of a big bank account?"

"Old age."

"Ha. When I get too old to take care of myself, I'll put a bullet through my head."

"Next time we get a suicide, I'll give you a call. You can come take a look."

"Gruesome? Maybe for you. He's out of his misery."

"Do me a favor, Jerry. Let me use this office for a few minutes."

"You want to make a call?"

"I have to interview somebody."

Jerry looked about the office, then shrugged and got to his feet. "Be my guest."

"There's a man out there in a corner booth named Findley. Tell him I'd like to see him."

"Promise you won't empty the safe."

"Go shoot yourself in the head."

Jerry closed the door after him and Horvath sat at the desk. He turned off the TV. He wasn't up to the Cubs. Who was? Jerry, apparently, and Wolmer. On the wall were framed photographs of the Cubs players. And managers. The one of Leo Durocher was signed. The door opened.

"He says go to hell."

"Is he still there?"

"He has half a drink he doesn't want to part with."

Horvath came out of the office and saw Findley standing by his booth, draining his glass. Horvath was beside him before Findley put the glass down.

"Come on into the office." He had Findley by his skinny elbow.

"Buzz off, Horvath. You want to talk with me, make an appointment."

"I may make an arrest."

Findley laughed. Small ferret face, long concave nose, it was hard to remember him as a cop. "I know the routines, Horvath. Remember? Take your hand off me."

"You want to go in, Findley? You really want that? It can be arranged. I want to talk to you about George Connolly. I want to know why you've been following me around all afternoon."

Findley's pride was hurt. He must really think he had kept out of sight. "You were hanging around Connolly's house, you were hanging around his office, you've been tailing me while I investigate a crime. Now that looks very strange, Findley. So you've got a choice. Wolmer's office or mine."

If there is a way to be defeated with dignity Findley had yet to master it. "I'm going to have another drink."

"Order it. You're going to need it."

Jerry said he would bring it into the office. Inside, Horvath pointed to the chair beneath the photo of Durocher. He settled behind the desk.

"A private investigator is legally bound to communicate to the police any and all information relevant to a crime."

"Don't tell me about private investigators, Horvath." Findley crossed his legs and tried to get comfortable in the chair, but it was a straightback and his effort was unrewarded.

"So what do you have to report about the death of George Connolly?"

"Connolly's dead, is he?"

"Tell me you were hired as security at his house with instructions to follow all shady characters, of which I am one."

"I don't do security work, Horvath."

"Don't give up, Findley. You may make it yet."

A knock on the door. Jerry thrust in a tray with Findley's martini on it. "How about you, Lieutenant? Want another beer?"

[84]

"I have to keep my wits about me while I interrogate this suspect."

Jerry stared at Findley who gave him the finger. "Horvath has all the wits in the department."

Having returned Findley's salute, Jerry closed the door.

"How did Connolly die?" Findley asked.

"Buy a paper."

"I've read the paper."

"Then you know as much as I do. About that. Tell me about Connolly."

"What would I know about Connolly? He's not a client of mine."

"Who you working for?"

"You know I don't have to tell you that."

"A private investigator is legally bound to communicate to the police any and all information relevant to a crime."

"I don't have any."

"Why were you hanging around Connolly's house?"

Findley sipped his drink. His expression invited Horvath to share his amazement at the universe. "I had no idea Connolly even lived in that neighborhood. I was there on another matter. In the neighborhood. I had a place staked out and it has nothing to do with Connolly. I saw you drive up to the house, not the one I was watching, and go in. So I turned on the radio and heard about Connolly. Now that wasn't very considerate of you, Horvath. Mrs. Connolly might have learned about her husband on the radio."

"You're going to lose your license."

"I'm telling you the truth."

"No, you're not. When I prove it, you're through. Why did you follow me?"

"Curiosity. I became convinced I was on a bad scent, so I thought I'd see what you were up to. You never know. There might be something for me in this Connolly murder."

"Like what?"

"Like I don't know. Things turn up. You have to be disposable."

"Disponible."

"What's the difference?"

"Ask your garbage man."

"So that's it. You want a statement, I'll make a statement."

"You do that, Findley. You just take yourself over to the department and make that statement. And be sure to sign it. It will come in useful at your license hearing."

"Anything to help the authorities in the investigation of a crime." Findley stood. He held the stem of his glass with two fingers and a thumb, his little finger curled beneath the base. "Is that all, Lieutenant?"

"I'm going to put a tail on you, Findley. Just to show you how it's done."

"Go to hell."

"See you in church."

Findley slammed the door when he went out. Horvath wondered if he should put a tail on Findley. He wouldn't mind doing the job himself, but it would be a silly game, hide and seek with an ex-cop. Findley no longer had an office and Horvath doubted if he had any records that would be helpful. He had always been behind with reports as a cop and when he did turn them in they were pretty bad. He had a knack for getting names and dates wrong and for missing the significant detail. Findley was a pariah, a cop who had quit, and then hung around to get in the way, a dismal reminder of ineptitude. Still, it was hard not to feel sorry for him. Findley must spend half his waking hours regretting his resignation.

Horvath got to his feet. There was no point in postponing his report to Keegan.

13

THE NURSE answered the door of the Connolly house and Keegan was glad that Dowling had agreed to come with him. The woman's eyes went to Dowling's collar and she stepped back to admit them without so much as a discouraging word.

"Thank God you're here, Father. This is the worst time."

"Where is she?"

"Father Dowling?" The voice came from the living room. No lights were on there, the drapes were drawn, and, standing in the front hall, Keegan and Dowling had to peer into the unlit room before they saw Mrs. Connolly. She had apparently been lying on the couch. Now she sat on its edge, an afghan over her shoulders, her eyes hollow and staring. Keegan followed Dowling in to her.

"Your housekeeper told the nurse she wasn't sure you could come."

"You called Mrs. Murkin?"

"Is that her name? I had to talk to you." Mrs. Connolly's eyes went to Keegan in an unstated question. He told her who he was.

"Please, Captain. Not now."

Dowling turned to him and Keegan nodded. He could talk to the nurse until Mrs. Connolly was ready for him. He found her in the kitchen, shoes off, a cup of coffee on the table before her.

"Help yourself, if you want a cup. I'm ready to drop."

"Hasn't she been unconcious?"

"Until an hour ago. But the phone hasn't stopped ringing." She shuddered. "I never realized how many creeps there are in the world. They must have thought I was Mrs. Connolly. The dreadful things they say!"

Keegan found a cup and poured himself some coffee. He sat across from the nurse. "What's your name?"

"Agnes. Agnes Daly. I guess I'm out of practice. I used to be at Saint Mary's, in surgery, but I quit nursing. I thought special nursing would be a breeze. We always thought it was. I'd rather spend all day in the operating room than go through another day like this."

Keegan looked at her. It was possible that one of those crank calls could be significant, but he hated to ask Mrs. Daly to repeat them. He explained to her why he had to ask.

She sighed, picked up her cup, then put it back in the saucer. "Most of them were, well, religious in a crazy way. She was being punished or her husband was being punished. They didn't make much sense. Sometimes just a burst of babble and they'd hang up."

"No names?"

"They were all anonymous."

"Did they mention anyone besides Mr. and Mrs. Connolly?"

[88]

"He did."

"He?"

"He was different. Cool. Very cool. I thought at first that he was a reporter. They've been calling too, when they haven't come to the door. One actually walked in the back way before I locked it. He had to have a story."

"This caller was a man," Keegan prompted.

"Yes. And very precise, if you know what I mean."

"Effeminate?"

"A little."

"What did he say? Try to remember exactly."

Mrs. Daly had both hands around her cup. She might have been warming them. "He said: 'Christ fell a second time but he rose from the dead.' Then he repeated it. It was weird. He seemed to say it as if it were something I had to understand."

"Was that all?"

"Does it mean anything?"

"I doubt it," Keegan lied. A vague troubling thought occurred to him, one he would like to discuss with Roger Dowling.

There was no point in burdening Mrs. Daly with it, but clearly, unless it was just a coincidence, one male caller with the precise, perhaps effeminate voice, had known the spot where Connolly was killed. Had that gotten into the newspapers? Keegan did not relish reading newspaper accounts of cases he was working on. When they weren't imaginative variations on the thin version he had given out, they were collections of irrelevancies and inaccurate facts. A reporter's purpose and a policeman's differ, much as fiction and truth do, but then the truth is not always entertaining.

"Are you staying all night?"

"My relief is due at nine. I was supposed to be relieved at six. Believe me, my husband is not going to look with favor on hours like these. I only hope that he insists I quit. Or go back to the hospital."

"Who's the doctor?"

"Mrs. Connolly's? Simmons."

"Has he been back?"

"His office phoned. She wanted a priest. Thank God she didn't answer any of those calls. It's enough to shake your faith to find what religion means to some people."

"Do the Connollys belong to Saint Hilary's?"

"They're supposed to. I gather they haven't gone in years. She was scared to death to call the priest, but she was more scared not to."

"Why so urgent? She won't have to make the funeral arrangements herself, will she?"

"Her sister and brother-in-law are coming in from Detroit later tonight."

"Did any of those callers mention Dolores?"

"Dolores who?"

"Just Dolores."

Mrs. Daly shook her head. Thank God she was too tired to be curious. Well, it had been a long shot anyway.

"Did Mrs. Connolly have much to say when she came out of it?"

Mrs. Daly rolled her eyes. That was answer enough. "The poor thing. But what can you say to someone whose husband has been . . ." Her lips formed the word, but she did not say it aloud.

"I wonder if there are any children."

"No children."

"Never were?"

"She didn't mention any."

Who was Dolores? Anyone at all? It would be nice to think that doodles are always meaningful. Perhaps they are, to a psychiatrist. The printed name in Connolly's notebook need bear no relation to anything else. It bore no perceptible relation to any of the notes he had taken on Placidus's conferences. Still, the somber thoughts induced by a retreat might have led on to other somber thoughts, to memories and thwarted hopes. The very name Dolores was sad. Dowling had wondered if the printed name was in Connolly's hand. That would be difficult to prove one way or the other, but it was a question Keegan had put to the lab. Printing is a disguise of sorts. To the naked eye, the name had been printed with the same ballpoint, apparently the one they had found in the drawer of the desk from which Pius had taken the notebook. A ballpoint pen with Assisi House embossed on it. Connolly had been carrying neither pen nor pencil when he died. Or at least when his body was found.

"Is coffee made?" It was Dowling, standing in the doorway.

"I'll take it to her," Keegan said. "Is she ready for me?"

"Captain Keegan, who could possibly be ready for you?" Dowling crossed the room and introduced himself to Agnes Daly. Things had gone rather quickly at the door when they had come in. "You must be exhausted."

"It's my job, Father. Would you like a cup of coffee? Sit down, sit down. I'll get it for you."

Mrs. Connolly had folded the afghan and placed it beside her on the couch. Her hair looked more tended to and there were several lights on in the room. Keegan explained who he was and why he must ask her what he knew would be painful questions.

"When did you last see your husband, Mrs. Connolly?"

She had taken a cigarette from a box on the table beside her. Keegan lit it for her. She seemed to expect him to.

[91]

"Saturday morning, when he left for Assisi House. We had breakfast together."

"And that was the last you spoke to him?"

"He said he wouldn't be calling home. He wasn't sure there was a phone there."

"And he didn't come home again?"

"Wasn't he killed there, at Assisi House? He had been there since Saturday."

"You've had time to think of this now. Was there anything at all that might have suggested what happened to your husband last night?"

She shook her head. "He was a very positive man, Captain. He was hard on people. But he always had been. There wasn't anything unusual lately."

"But you're saying he had enemies?"

She dragged on her cigarette before agreeing. "I suppose every successful man leaves a trail of victories behind him. And if someone wins, someone else loses."

"Business was good?"

"Oh, wonderful." But she stopped herself. "As far as I know. I guess I really don't know. It always has been. Is something wrong at the plant?"

"No trouble between the two of you?"

"Certainly not."

"How long have you been married?"

"It will be thirty-five years in . . ." Except that it would not. She and George would celebrate no more anniversaries. It was the kind of realization she would keep on having for a time, another stab of pain, more tears.

"Why didn't he drive his own car to Assisi House?"

"They were going in a group. He rented a minibus."

"Your husband did?"

"Yes. That is, I gather he did. Didn't he?"

"I don't know. What group was it, by the way?"

Again she didn't know. He could see that she was getting the sensation of not doing terribly well in an exam and, since the topic was her life, or her husband's life, she began to grow annoyed.

"How often did your husband make retreats at Assisi House?"

"Not very often."

"When was the last time?"

"I'm not sure."

"Then it wasn't recently?"

"Captain, George was an extremely busy man. For him to get away for a day or two was all but impossible."

"Were any of the men with him at Assisi House men over whom he had won those victories you mentioned?"

"Do you mean, were they his enemies?"

"Yes."

"I don't know who was in the group. Exactly," she added.

Keegan took out his notebook and read the names to her. There was not much reaction until he came to Leahy.

"Maurice Leahy? We haven't seen him in years."

"Old friends?"

"Yes." A soft light came into her eyes. "That was nice, asking Maurice."

"It surprises you?"

"George was not a very forgiving person."

"What would he have to forgive Maurice Leahy?"

"I don't even remember, it was so long ago. All I remember is that George was furious with Maurice. For a time, he feared that . . ." Again she stopped. "It's no good my pretending I understand the least thing about George's business, Captain. I don't. I never did. But it was some business thing that was at the bottom of their falling out."

"How long ago was this?"

"Oh, years ago."

"Twenty years ago, ten years ago?"

"Closer to ten than to twenty."

"Your husband was already in business for himself?"

"Yes, I think so."

"What about these others, Marston, Wolmer . . ."

"I've heard of Marston. Isn't he a banker?"

"A lawyer. What of the others? Wolmer, Crispi, Browner."

"We had an insurance man named Browner."

"Mr. Browner sells insurance."

"The others I just don't remember. Perhaps I should, but I don't."

"Tell me when the idea of a retreat first came up."

"I don't know. The first I heard of it was on Friday, the day before George left. He just announced it. At first I was furious, but then I could see it was a good idea." She started to cry again. "Thank God he was there when it happened. If it had to happen. We haven't been very religious, George and I."

"Who is Dolores?"

"What?"

"Dolores."

"I don't know any Dolores." The tears had stopped.

Keegan put his notebook back into his pocket. "Is Mrs. Leahy's name Dolores?"

"No. Where did you get that idea?"

"Neither you nor your husband knew anyone named Dolores?"

"I've already answered that, Captain."

She was lying. A watchful look had entered her widened eyes. The sound of Mrs. Daly and Father Dowling talking in the kitchen came to them, a reassuring murmur. Keegan stood.

"Thank you, Mrs. Connolly. I'm sorry to have to bother you at a time like this."

"My sister from Detroit is coming, with her husband."
She seemed to want to say that she was not alone. "Would you
ask Father Dowling if I could speak to him again?"

Keegan had another cup of coffee with Agnes Daly.
Her replacement came, a pudgy little woman with dyed red
hair who looked around as if she were taking permanent
possession of the house. She was not sympathetic to Mrs. Daly's
account of her trying day. Her name was Schiller and she was
anxious to meet her charge. She refused a cup of coffee but she
opened the refrigerator and looked over its contents. Keegan
had the feeling that this house would keep few secrets from
Miss Schiller. He would have to tell Horvath to sit down with
Miss Schiller after she had spent a little time in the house.

The voices from the living room were audible, clearly
no confidence was being imparted. Keegan suggested to Mrs.
Daly that she take Miss Schiller in to meet Mrs. Connolly.
This had the result of prying Dowling loose. Dowling wasn't
likely to admit it, but Keegan had the feeling, as they walked
out to the car, that the pastor of St. Hilary's was happy
enough to be heading back to Assisi House.

"Was she any help?" Dowling asked.

"I'm not sure."

But this was not the point for certainties. Keegan
wished that there was time for a long conversation with Dowling, leisurely, trying unlikely hypotheses. The Connolly home
had been an unhappy one but Keegan did not find that
surprising. Only his own remembered marriage seemed flaw-
less to him. But there was more than an unhappy marriage
behind Connolly's death, and that more had something to do
with the religious setting in which it had occurred. And that
was Dowling's department. But he could not burden Roger
with this, any more than he already was. The man was supposed to be on retreat.

14

MAURICE LEAHY sat on a bench under an apple tree, smoking
a cigar and drinking Scotch, two habits he had been warned
against for the past quarter of a century. George Connolly's
violent death had made him even more disdainful of such
cautionary advice. Sixty years old. Bim had bet him he would
never make it to fifty and he had buried her three years ago.
He would end up burying the undertaker. Mellowed by the
Scotch, he marveled at his ability to be unmoved by death, by
Bim's, by Connolly's, by dozens of others in recent years. Bim
had gone swiftly. She had been having check-ups twice a year
for as long as he could remember. She died of cancer six weeks
after getting a clean bill of health. Maurice had wanted to sue
that sonofabitch of a doctor but he couldn't find a lawyer that
he cared to hire who would take the case. Just as well. It
would have been pretty ghoulish turning a profit on Bim's

death. He himself was insurance poor and what they had carried on Bim barely got her into the ground. Bim and now George Connolly.

What a way to go. Had it been painful? It had to be. An ice pick in the chest. God. But it must have been quick, anyway. What surprised Leahy was that death did not turn his thoughts to the sort of things old Placidus had been haranguing them about. All day George had provided a text for the morbid Franciscan. Like a thief in the night, he whispered over their heads. We know not the day nor the hour. What did they do here, knock off one in every group to scare the rest? It hadn't been any thief who got George Connolly in the night.

Leahy slapped at a mosquito. Greedy little bastards, went right for the ankles. High above him the summer sky wheeled slowly. He put back his head and looked at the stars. That is all they were to him, stars. He had been fifty before he realized that stars actually move, that the summer and winter sky differ. All he saw were points of light in an inky darkness. No thoughts of impossible reaches of space, the insignificance of earth and man. Just a sky that had been there when he was a kid and would still be there when he was forgotten. He felt no stab of regret at the realization. He had long since stopped thinking the universe was interested in him. What the hell, he was small potatoes in Fox River, Illinois! Always had been and always would be. So what? He was alive and breathing, enjoying a cigar and some halfway decent Scotch. George Connolly had been big potatoes and that hadn't helped him much last night. It might have been what had done him in.

The buzz of the house was who did it? It seemed to Maurice Leahy that the problem was not a dearth of candidates but their number. He himself had had reason to put an ice pick into George. For all he knew, the four others on this crazy retreat had equal reason. He wouldn't be surprised if it turned out to be one of the four who had done it. They had been the same age, he and George. Bim had always liked Lucille Connolly. Especially when she found out what an asshound George Connolly was. Then Bim could pity Lucille and not feel intimidated by her lofty manner. George had still been at it, Maurice was sure of that. The cops must have figured out by now that George had slipped out of the house last night. Beat it right after supper as far as Leahy could figure it out.

Leahy's cigar glowed in the night as he dragged on it. What a noisy place the country is. Cicadas whirring away like power tools, the sound of faraway traffic, the barking of dogs carried eerily on the night air. And the damned mosquitoes. He crossed his legs and slapped at his ankle. Where had George gone last night? When Keegan knew that he would have solved the case.

A car turned in the road and Leahy went rigid as the lights swept over him. The car tires crunched when they left the blacktop and entered the parking lot. Lights out, motor off, the sound of doors opening. They slammed shut again. Voices. How close they seemed. Had they noticed him? He cupped his cigar in his hand.

It was Keegan and the priest. Dowling. It had been stupid to lie to Keegan about Connolly, about St. Hilary's, for Christ's sake, with the present pastor sitting right there. At least they hadn't called him on it. Leahy shook his head sadly. Had he thought they would be impressed by the story that he and George Connolly were friends?

Dowling was pointing toward the sky and saying something to Keegan. The priest looked like some mad prophet drawing attention to a sign of the times. Keegan looked about as interested as Leahy would have been.

The two men went inside, leaving the night to Maurice Leahy.

He dragged on his cigar, took another sip of Scotch. Ah. The good life. He had quit pretending he was still interested in women. The year after Bim died . . . He shook away the thoughts. He had no regrets.

He had been sitting out here last night too. Hot days, cool nights. After the euchre game, the rest of them yawned and scratched and trailed away to bed. Not that Leahy had been all that anxious to share his booze with any of them. Connolly might not have been so bad. After he got his bottle, he stopped at George's room and knocked. No answer. He hadn't expected one really. The rooms were all alike. George had stranded them here, hiring that minibus to bring them, but he had managed to get away himself. How? With whom? A notebook lay on the desk. Leahy read it with a smile. Who the hell did George think he was kidding? George Connolly getting religion? That was a laugh. So he had taken up the pen and printed *Dolores* in the book. If George wanted food for meditation, that name should be a help.

A wasted gesture. George had never returned to his room. It was just as well. It wouldn't have taken him very long to figure out who had printed Dolores in that notebook.

15

THANK God Jimmy was in bed and asleep when the police called. Caroline Perth had taken her son to a movie, had sat through it numb and unseeing, not wanting to think, unable to be distracted. Home again, she put Jimmy in bed and had just taken a sleeping pill herself when the bell rang. She had read somewhere that the smell of pastry had been the basis on which Proust had recalled his childhood and youth in infinite detail, the past coming back whole and entire on the wings of a scarcely remembered odor. She believed it. Her own memory was much the same. Tactile, olfactory, and, as her reaction to the sound of the bell proved, audial as well. And with the memory came the childhood fear of ghosts. The bell rang again. She had to answer it. The sound would waken Jimmy.

She had the safety chain on, of course. George had insisted on that. He liked to think of her and Jimmy as vulnerable. But she did not even open the door. "Who is it?" she called.

"Police."

O Lord. She opened the door but it was not Lieutenant Horvath. The little man opened and closed his wallet to reveal a badge.

"It's late," she complained.

"I'm sorry, ma'am, I have to talk to you. Something has come up."

She looked at him. He wasn't very imposing. Finally she nodded, closing the door to undo the chain. He came in, crossed the room to a chair, and sat down. He looked around the room in appraisal.

"Very nice."

"Thank you."

"Please sit down, Mrs. Perth."

"I told Lieutenant Horvath all I know that could possibly be of help."

He looked up at her, saying nothing. She sat down.

He said, "You failed to mention the nature of your relationship to Mr. Connolly."

"What do you mean?"

"Don't, Mrs. Perth. Let's not waste our time." He opened a notebook. "Shall we start with April? On April seven you went in the company of Mr. Connolly to the Hilton hotel in Chicago."

"Who told you that?"

"April thirty, the Holiday Inn, Elgin, Illinois." He fluttered the pages of his notebook. "Shall I go on?"

"What do you want? This has nothing to do with anything."

"I doubt that Mrs. Connolly would agree."

"Why would you tell her? Now?"

"I wouldn't."

He was completely different from Lieutenant Horvath. He sat there smiling at her in a conspiratorial way. "What's your name?" she demanded.

"I'll ask the questions."

"You're not asking questions. You're just saying things. I don't believe you're from the police at all." The thought brought her to her feet.

"I'm not."

"Who are you?"

She moved, getting between him and the hall that led to Jimmy's bedroom. "You get out of here. You said you were from the police."

"Take it easy. I'm a detective. A private detective. My name is Findley. Sit down, I'm not going to bite you."

"A private detective." She sat down. What a disgusting little snoop he was. "Did she hire you?"

"Never mind who hired me," he snapped. "Lady, you're in real trouble. Let's get that clear. Don't you get the picture? I know every move you and Connolly have made since last April."

"Is that when you began spying on me?"

"That's when I began."

"Why? What did she have to gain?"

"Mrs. Connolly? She had something to lose, didn't she? Like a husband."

She wanted to shout *No!* It was the truth. She had stopped believing George was going to get a divorce and marry her. It had been a ridiculous thought anyway, he had never promised a thing. He was nearly thirty years older than she, older than her own father would have been, but it had been hard to let go of the thought that he meant to marry her. That would have been less ridiculous than sneaking around to hotels and motels with a man his age. When she stopped thinking that marriage would be the end of it, she was left with the realization that she was George's mistress. And it didn't help that he was good to her, gave her things, paid her twice what she was worth to him as a secretary, gave her to that degree a sense of security. She was just his mistress with no real claim on him. And he was getting old. It couldn't go on much longer. He hadn't wanted to talk of that. It had been strange being with someone for whom the future did not exist, not any future that contained them or what they did. Whenever he got sentimental he talked of what it would have been like if he had known her years ago, but the time he was speaking of was a time when she had been a little girl or had not been at all. In place of a future that would not be he had a past that had not been. It was like hoping backward. Maybe most hopes for the future are just as silly. Certainly hers had been.

The little creep Findley sat watching her adjust to the thought that he knew all about her and George, at least since April. It was eerie to realize that someone had been spying on them all those months, watching, observing, keeping a record. Why? It really made no sense. As far as she could figure out, George and his wife had come to an understanding years ago. Caroline had no illusion that she was the first. In fact that had been part of his line at the beginning, as if he had known it would be easier for her if she knew other younger women had found him attractive. She had thought he was kidding. Old guys liked to jolly about sex, but it was usually all talk. Most of them would die of fright if you took them halfway seriously. But George had meant it and he had taken his time, as if he had all the time in the world, and from preposterous it had become possible, first remotely possible, then plausible, until she had thought, why not? He was her boss. It couldn't hurt her job security. But when the pay raises started she had had the awful recognition that she was being *paid*, and she knew what that made her. She had actually broken off with him, quit her job, started looking for another. That was when she realized how swiftly she had become dependent on the unusual salary George paid her. But it had not been the money alone that brought her back. He had been sweet and patient and understanding. She knew he could be a perfect bastard to the men in the shop, but the side of him she saw was the side she wanted to think was the real George.

"Have you told the police about me?"

He shook his head.

"Are you going to?"

"That depends."

She was used to his smirk by now. Had she ever caught a glimpse of him before? It seemed impossible that someone could sneak around spying on you for months and you wouldn't notice. But of course she had never dreamed such a thing was going on. She wanted to think she must have noticed him. Now, after the first shock, she began to think Findley was someone she could handle.

"Mr. Findley, what if I should call the police right now and tell them everything you know?"

"Go ahead."

"I don't know what you think knowing about George and me makes you, but I'll tell you. It makes you a sneak. I don't care if Mrs. Connolly paid you to do it. It is a lousy way to make a living."

"You can say that again."

"Why do you do it?"

"Because it is a living."

"What earthly good will it do if the police know about me? What good did it do Mrs. Connolly?"

"She doesn't know."

Caroline stared at him. Findley was suddenly less harmless than he had seemed a moment ago. "You didn't even give her what she paid for?"

"Did I say she was paying me? No. You said that."

"Then who?"

His smile was evil, there was no other word for it. Her mind went in a dozen directions at once but she had no idea at all who besides Mrs. Connolly could possibly have had any reason for following her.

"What do you want?"

"Knowledge is power, Caroline. Do you know the saying? I've imagined talking to you, do you know that? It is a strange thing to know so much about another person when they are not even aware that you exist. I've thought of you as Caroline from the start. Well, finally, here we are. Of course the circumstances are not what I had imagined. Poor Connolly."

"It was you!"

"Who killed Connolly?" Findley laughed, a dreadful laugh. "Not on your life, lady."

"But you know who did."

Again the smile. She couldn't tell whether it was swagger or not. Oh, she knew the type, she hated the type, her skin crawled to have him in her apartment. But how was she going to get him out?

"I know and you know where Connolly was last night. The police would very much like to know that."

"Then tell them!"

"Should I? Think of your son, Caroline. Have you any idea what the police would do with a prize like you? The questions, the publicity, and then the testifying. You wouldn't have an hour to call your own for months, for a year. Of course you would start off as a suspect. By the time they discounted that your name would be ruined. Your life would be a shambles."

"Stop it."

"Then you've got the picture? Good."

"What do you want, money? I don't have money."

"No money."

"You know so much about me, you must know that. I can't give you a thing."

He looked at her, unsmiling now, somehow more creepy.

"We'll think of something, Caroline. Don't worry. We'll think of something."

16

Two RECEIVERS lifted in the middle of the first ring and both Mrs. Murkin and Bovril cried hello.

"Hello," Dowling said. "Is that you, Marie?"

"Father Dowling!"

"This is Father Bovril," Bovril said firmly. "Hello."

"I'll talk to Marie, Father. Perhaps we can have a word in a few minutes."

"Is that Father Dowling?"

"That's right."

"You'll be happy to hear that everything is shipshape here. How is the retreat going?"

"Well, there's only been one murder."

"Murder!"

"I read all about it in the paper," Marie chirped. "Isn't that eerie, that happening, and the very night you got there?"

"I didn't do it, Marie."

"Oh, Father."

"Marie, perhaps if I had a few words with Father Bovril first then we could have a little chat."

"Sure, Father. That's okay." She sounded as if they shared a secret. The sound of the extension in the rectory kitchen being hung up came along the line.

"Father Bovril?"

"Still here." Bovril's voice was a little strained and aloof. Clearly he did not like to vie with the housekeeper, but just as clearly he was willing to, if it came to that. "Mrs. Murkin is, in the phrase, a jewel."

"Isn't she? Father, there will be a funeral tomorrow for George Connolly. The arrangements will be made through McGinnis."

"How do you spell Connolly?"

"Oh, there's nothing you must do. It may not be tomorrow. It depends on when the police release the body."

"The police."

"He was murdered."

"Good Lord."

"Here at Assisi House. That's what Marie was talking about."

"I haven't had time to look at a paper or watch the news since I got here."

"Really?" Bovril had arrived on Sunday at eight o'clock. "You've been keeping pretty busy?"

Bovril sighed. "I've got an organist for the noon Mass today."

"An organist."

"I have absolute pitch myself but I find it unwise to count on that in others. Besides, an organ tempts people into song. I had a rather inert bunch yesterday."

"My regulars. You'll find them devout and pious but undemonstrative. I just offer Mass for them. That is what they've come for. A very simple Mass. And to say their prayers."

"I know. There were several rosaries banging against the pews during the liturgy yesterday."

"Don't do anything daring, Father."

"I'd thought of inviting someone to come up and do the readings."

"I wouldn't."

"You don't do that?"

"No, I don't. Just say Mass for them, Father."

"I realize they're probably a conservative little clique, but I have found that even reactionaries respond to a zestfully done liturgy."

Father Dowling turned in the chair behind Cyprian's desk and looked out across the front lawn of Assisi House. There seemed to be a bottle beneath a bench out there. There was little point in arguing with Bovril. The man could not do too much harm in a week. But this conversation did settle one thing.

"I'll be saying the funeral Mass myself, of course. I'll take the wake at McGinnis's too."

"There's no need to do that."

"I think the widow expects it. It's really no trouble."

"This fellow was actually murdered?"

"No doubt about it."

"That's hard to believe."

"It happens all the time, Father. Incidentally, have you ever come across a young Franciscan named Blaise? I don't know if he's a priest or a brother."

"Blaise. Not in our province. Young, you say?"

"About your age."

"Certainly no one that young. We're not taking those odd names at profession any more. We retain our baptismal names."

"I see." Bovril's baptismal name was Marion. "He was here at Assisi House Sunday night."

"One of the men there should be able to tell you who he is."

"They don't seem to know him either."

"That's odd. Haven't they spoken to him?"

"I seem to be the only one who saw him."

"He's left then?"

"I met him in the chapel and then he seems to have disappeared."

"Perhaps it was an apparition."

"Who was Saint Blaise?"

"Damned if I know."

"The feast is on February second," Dowling recalled. "At least it used to be. Remember, we blessed throats."

"Blessed throats?"

Surely Bovril couldn't be that young. It seemed only yesterday that one had come out again after Mass on February second and passed along the communion railing with two lit crossed candles, holding them under the throats of those kneeling there and praying that they would be spared what? He wasn't too sure. The memory had an aura to it he was sure Bovril would deprecate. How swiftly things had changed. Imagine a priest who had no memory of the blessing of

[109]

throats, not even as a child. But then Bovril probably knew no Latin either. Dowling had a most vivid memory of the first priest he had met who had never studied Latin. He had felt swept back into a pre-Tridentine clerical incompetence. The man had been newly ordained, scarcely more than twenty-five, and he actually preened himself on his ignorance of Latin. What was the need of it, now that the liturgy was in the vernacular? No more hocus pocus, he had said with a grin. Perhaps he thought it was a Latin phrase. Dowling had thought of the vast patrimony that was closed to the youthful cleric: he was a man of the present, of the moment, ahistorical, untouched by and uninterested in tradition. Dowling dreaded to think what parodies of the past might be floating about within that youthful sacerdotal head. He was half tempted to find out now if Bovril knew Latin, but that would be cruel. Dowling had retained the authors he had read in school, the very copies he had pored over as a boy and young man, Caesar, Vergil, Horace, and Tacitus. Catullus too, an improbable author to be read by a seminarian. But then the same might have been said of Lucretius. Augustine and then Aquinas had dulled the edge of his classical Latin, but Dowling was not one of those who regarded medieval Latin condescendingly. He subscribed to the view of C. S. Lewis, who had been unimpressed by Renaissance attempts to revive the classical style. Such authors had written a closet Latin, it was they who had embalmed it and left it dead, whereas medieval Latin had been a living tongue, altered precisely because it was alive. Men had spoken it, thought in it, written it with verve and directness.

"We used to church women too," Dowling said to Bovril, although that practice had died out before his own time. "A lovely liturgy. Let me speak to Mrs. Murkin, will you, Father?"

"How do I do that?"

"Just punch the red button on your phone."

"Yes?" Marie had obviously been waiting to get back on.

"Well, good-by," Bovril said and hung up.

Marie's sigh was prolonged and eloquent.

"Things going all right, Marie?"

"I'll survive. I've never felt like a servant before."

"Oh?"

"He *orders* his meals. Last night he actually handed me a recipe. A rice dish. Was he in the missions or something?"

"It's only for a week."

"Tell me about the murder."

To cheer her up? "Well, someone drove an ice pick into the man's chest. I found the body. They have outdoor stations of the cross here and on Monday morning I woke very early and went outside and there he was."

"George Connolly."

"He'll be buried from Saint Hilary's. I spoke with Mrs. Connolly yesterday. I'd never met either of them before."

"How could you?"

"What do you mean?"

"Neither one of them has been in church for years."

"At Saint Hilary's. Perhaps they went somewhere else."

"Perhaps." But Marie's voice was heavy with doubt. "You know, there was some gossip about him, years ago. I gather he wasn't the best of husbands. Maybe it's something they stayed together."

Mrs. Connolly had hinted at marital difficulties when he had talked with her last night, though she had not wanted to paint too black a picture of her husband. At the same time, she had wanted assurance that he had been in an appropriate

[111]

moral condition when he died, given the fact that he was on retreat at Assisi House. She seemed to think a few days there should offset a lifetime of dalliance. Of course, Dowling knew nothing of the man and had no desire in any case to get involved in any celestial handicapping. He had told Mrs. Connolly that she could be confident of the divine mercy, though of course God is a just God. It was the ultimate mystery, really, human freedom. People spoke of God condemning souls to hell or according them heaven, but it is our free choices that determine our ultimate and eternal condition. Not even God can force our will. Nor is He likely to make a mockery of our freedom by dismissing the self we have constructed over a lifetime and rewarding and punishing us independently of who we are. Fortunately, Mrs. Connolly had not been the kind of bereaved relative who insists on getting into a theological argument.

"We quarreled a lot, Father. We quarreled on the day he left."

"Most married people quarrel, Mrs. Connolly."

"Ours was not a good marriage."

He said nothing. He did not relish such confidences, but it was difficult to refuse her the right to talk now.

"My first thought, when they told me he was dead, was that I was responsible."

"You must not think that."

"There were times when I wished him dead, Father. I am sure he wished the same for me."

Was such hatred possible in marriage? A cynic might say it is only possible in marriage. Dowling hoped Mrs. Connolly was being hyperbolic. It was a chilling thought that strangers, let alone spouses, can wish one another evil.

"Sometimes it was almost like a prayer. Is George's death the answer to my prayer?"

"Surely you're not glad he's dead."

"No."

"Then you did not really wish him dead."

"If we hadn't been Catholics, we would have divorced."

The marriage vows are a lifetime promise, but Mrs. Connolly made them sound rather like a life sentence. And the point of the permanency is fidelity and love. Another topic he did not want to go into with her, not now. Whatever her marriage had been, it was unchangeable now.

"You must pray for him now. That is the best thing you can do for him. If you feel you were less than a good wife to him alive, make up for it now."

"The failure was not exactly on my side, Father."

Was she still trying to win an argument with her dead husband? Dowling turned the conversation to the funeral arrangements and that somber topic brought back the tears. He preferred having her weep. It seemed a more promising basis from which to review her marriage, if that is what she wished to do.

"I haven't been to Mass in years, Father."

"Would you like to go to confession?"

"I scarcely remember how."

"It's just a matter of talking. Now is as good a time as any."

"Right here?"

He nodded. This was one grace she received from her husband's brutal death. He helped her recall her sins of commission and omission, he spoke of motives for contrition and remorse, he gave her absolution. He hoped this would indeed be a turning point for her. How empty a life can seem, how wasted, when it is recalled in the presence of God. Unlike her husband, Mrs. Connolly still had the opportunity to go on differently than she had until now.

Marie Murkin said, "The funeral will be here?"

"I'll come in to say the Mass."

[113]

"Good. Who knows what *he* might do at a funeral. Dance, maybe."

Dowling did not laugh. Marie's week would be bad enough without his encouraging her grumbling. He told her to keep the faith and that he would see her soon, perhaps tomorrow.

When he had hung up, he stood and looked out the window. Someone was mowing the lawn, a little tractor-mower looking even smaller under the large man riding it, the swath it cut an arm's breadth wide. The man went methodically back and forth. He seemed as dogged as Keegan on a case. Keegan was not at Assisi House. He had gone to his office after hearing Dowling's Mass, not even staying for breakfast. The house and grounds swarmed with his men. The trail from the parking lot to the seventh station was taped off and the outdoor stations were temporarily out of bounds. Marston was annoyed.

"I have acquired the habit of going down to the lake."

"Is that the only path?"

"It is the one I have always taken."

"Apparently Connolly came across that field to the path."

"If they already know that, what are they looking for?"

"He wasn't alone."

Marston's eyebrows lifted in comprehension. "I still find it difficult to believe it was right here that George . . ."

"The dead have a way of becoming memories very quickly. And where do memories exist?"

"Isn't that a bit heretical, Father?"

Marston relished the role of theologian. Dowling did not.

"Did Connolly ever mention Dolores to you?"

"Immortality is not merely a matter of being remembered, is it?"

Had Marston heard the question? Dowling repeated it.

"Who is she?"

"I don't know."

They were standing in the lobby where Dowling had run into Marston after coming out of Cyprian's office. Marston plucked a book from a wire rack. It was a life of St. Francis by Chesterton.

"Do you know this book, Father Dowling?"

"I enjoyed it. Almost it makes one like Franciscans. Of course that is not entailed by liking St. Francis."

"How has her name come up?" Marston had opened the book and was scanning a page.

"Apparently Connolly had printed it in his notebook."

"Apparently?"

"The name was printed there, but did Connolly do it?"

"Isn't that all rather mysterious? I mean these hypotheses and counterhypotheses."

"You think Connolly wrote her name there?"

"I think nothing one way or the other."

"I wonder who she is."

Marston looked at him. "Is it his wife's name?"

"No."

Marston shook his head. "If the police occupy themselves with things like that their investigation will go on forever."

"You don't think it has anything to do with his death?"

"Once more, Father Dowling, I think neither the one thing nor the other. No, that's not true. It sounds like a wild-goose chase to me."

"You're right."

Marston was surprised.

"I mean that murders seldom pose much of a puzzle. One doesn't have to go chasing about looking for who did it."

"Do the police have a suspect?"

"Oh, I should think so."

"I wonder who it is."

"Perhaps Dolores."

Marston frowned and closed the book. "I think I will buy this. Or is the man you mentioned yesterday here perhaps? Pascal?"

They looked together. Pascal was not to be found in the rack. Dowling was not surprised. Marston bought Chesterton's life of St. Francis. He seemed reluctant to leave Dowling but eventually he did. His step was not as brisk as it might have been. Dowling conjectured that this might have something to do with the mention of Dolores. The mention of the name in Connolly's notebook, that is. He could hardly mention the person named. He felt this was a distinction Marston would have appreciated.

17

WHEN PEANUTS called about Caroline Perth, Keegan told him not to do a thing, not to ask her any questions, not to answer any questions, just keep her there until he arrived. "Take her into my office, Peanuts. Make her comfortable. Get her coffee, rolls, whatever she wants. Cigarettes."

"Yessir." Peanuts was impressed by the effect his call was having.

"Have you told anyone else she's there?"

"No."

"Call Horvath. Tell him I want to see him."

"Should I tell him why?"

"You can tell Horvath. Tell him I want him there when I question her."

"Roger," Peanuts said and Keegan winced.

Keegan had heard Dowling's Mass distractedly, wondering if he shouldn't have skipped it and gotten into town.

With Peanuts, as with God, all things were possible. He could imagine arriving at his office and finding it stripped, Peanuts and the woman gone, not a clue in the world as to where they were. He was going to have to do something about Peanuts. Imagine letting that trail from the parking lot to the path be found by Dowling after the area had presumably been gone over by the police. Maybe they would all be better off with Peanuts on the city council with the rest of his benighted family.

Horvath was there when he arrived, waiting in the hall.

"Peanuts won't let me in to see her."

"Good. I mean for once he's doing what he was told to do."

"What's it all about?"

"Let's find out."

What it was all about was Findley. The woman wept as she told her story. Findley had been following her. He had found out that she was seeing a married man. He had come to her home and blackmailed her with the knowledge.

"How much money did you give him?"

"I don't have any money!"

She stared at Keegan with red eloquent eyes. Keegan understood with some embarrassment.

Peanuts said, "Findley was here yesterday."

"What was he doing here?"

"He'd heard about the Connolly killing."

"What time yesterday?"

"When you told me to take off. He wanted to know what we knew about Connolly's killing."

Horvath said to Caroline Perth, "The married man you were seeing was George Connolly, wasn't it?"

"Yes."

Keegan exploded. "Why the hell didn't you say so?"

[118]

Driving into town like a madman, Keegan had tried not to feel vindictive toward Findley, but it was difficult not to be glad that they finally had something on him. A woman ready to file a complaint. It was an old ambition, to get Findley's license and drive him from Fox River. He despised Findley for despising the force, particularly when Findley had been such a lousy cop himself. Now to find that the woman who wanted to bring charges against him was the mistress of the murdered man whose killer he sought! Much of the sympathy he had left for the woman had evaporated. Keegan was conscious of the jungle surrounding him.

"Horvath, go get him. I want him and I want him quick."

"He wanted the names of people we were checking out," Peanuts said.

"And you told him."

Peanuts looked bewildered. "I thought it would be in the paper anyway."

Horvath stopped in the doorway. "No wonder the bastard was tailing me all day."

"You let Findley tail you?"

"I didn't *let* him. I called him on it."

"Go get him, Horvath."

The door slammed. Keegan told Peanuts to get lost. "Bring some coffee." And then he was alone with the first solid lead he had in Connolly's death.

"All right, Mrs. Perth. Get comfortable. This is going to take a long time."

"But what about my little boy?"

"You're a mother?"

"Yes." Shame shone in her eyes.

"Did you bring him with you?"

"There's a baby sitter with him. I told her I wouldn't be long."

"Then let's get started. How long have you known George Connolly?"

"I've been working for him since last November. As a secretary."

She hadn't started as a secretary. Her predecessor hadn't liked working for Connolly and when she left Caroline Perth had a chance to move up. Or down, depending on your point of view. Keegan got the impression that she had understood the implications of the promotion from the first. She had never worked as a secretary before. But she insisted that she learned quickly, that she had carried her weight. What had she thought of George Connolly? She liked him. She said it half defiantly, as if she realized it was a minority opinion. He had been good to her, a lot better than he had had to be, a lot better than most men were. Was she thinking of Findley? Keegan half admired her loyalty. Only half. She was dumber than she looked, getting into a situation like that. She was an attractive woman, a mother besides, she should have known better than to get involved with someone Connolly's age. She couldn't possibly have thought it would lead to marriage. So what had she been after if not the money, no matter that it came in the form of a high salary and job security. Well, Keegan had never professed to understand women.

"When did you last see George Connolly?"

"He had been out of town."

"Do you know when he left town?"

"I think on Saturday."

"You saw him Friday?"

"Just for a little while."

"Did you go to work on Friday?"

"Oh. You mean at work."

"You saw him after work?"

"For an hour or so." Her eyes drifted away and her voice dropped, as if that would make her rendezvous with

[120]

Connolly less significant. He assumed it had been a rendezvous.

"Where?"

"What do you mean?"

"Did he come to your home?"

"No. This was early evening."

"Then you normally did not have your meetings at your home?"

"Captain, we met in motels and hotels all around here, and in Chicago. You name it, we were probably there. And this man Findley apparently began to follow us. He had places and dates."

"Did he say who he was working for?"

"He claimed it wasn't Mrs. Connolly."

"But you think it was?"

"Who else would it be?"

"Did Connolly ever give you any reason to think his wife suspected something was going on between you?"

"He almost never mentioned his wife."

"But you were secretive, you and Connolly?"

"No. We didn't flaunt ourselves, but, no, I didn't think we were being sneaky."

"How many people knew you were having an affair with him?"

The phrase seemed to startle, then to amuse her. "None."

"You mentioned it to none of your friends?"

"Of course not."

"Not even a hint?"

Her expression of annoyance was all the answer he got.

"Have you been going out with other men?"

"No."

"Exclusively with George Connolly. For how long?"

"I wasn't going out with anybody when I went to work for him."

She did not say it, but Keegan imagined a lonely woman, still young, with a child to support, with no contacts with eligible men. She must have seemed very ripe for the picking to Connolly.

"Who killed him, Mrs. Perth?"

The question brought her erect in her chair. "I don't know."

"You knew him as well as anybody, perhaps better than anyone else. A man tells a woman things. And you saw him all day at work. Who were his enemies?"

"He didn't have enemies. He was a businessman."

"All his employees are blissfully content?"

"Nooo. Of course there were complaints, but nothing serious."

"Who complained?"

"Men in the shop. Through the steward. Safety features they thought were inadequate, lighting, the ventilation. And of course they didn't like rush jobs."

"Was there anyone who complained more than the others?"

"Captain, it wasn't anybody at the plant. I'm sure of that. He was a hard man to work for but nobody hated him. If they did, they could go elsewhere. Tool and die men are in a sellers' market George always said. He seemed to think he was too lenient with the men in the shop and I suppose that was his explanation."

"Did you kill him?"

"Me!"

"Did you kill George Connolly?"

"No. He was . . . I . . . we were very good friends. I liked him. Why would I kill him?"

Keegan opened his hands. "Because he wouldn't leave his wife?"

"He never said he would. I never asked him to."

"Why not?"

"I don't know why not."

"Was this just a casual affair in your eyes?"

"No. I don't have casual affairs. I had never before been involved with a man like this."

"You mean, steady."

"I mean at all."

"Do you have a regular baby sitter?"

"Why do you ask that?"

"I gather you've spent much of the past year away from home in the company of George Connolly."

"We didn't go away for days, Captain."

"But overnight?"

"Often, yes."

"So you had a baby sitter?"

"Of course."

"The same one?"

"Captain, you aren't going to ask her questions, are you?"

"Where would you tell her you were going?"

"I said it was a business trip. I told her I represented the company at sales shows and that sort of thing. So she wasn't surprised that I was away a lot. She thought it was my job."

Keegan allowed a silence to form. Of course these trips must have been a large part of what Connolly was paying her for. The same thought seemed to have occurred to Caroline Perth.

"You knew that George Connolly had gone to a place called Assisi House to make a religious retreat?"

"He didn't tell me exactly where he was going."

"Or why?"

"No. What is a religious retreat?"

"It is a time when people think about their lives, pray,

assess themselves, try to see how they measure up to their ideal. He didn't mention this to you?"

"Not like that, no."

"Does it sound like the sort of thing George Connolly might do?"

She shook her head slowly. "No."

"Then what do you suppose he was doing there?"

"Is that all he could have been doing there?"

"What do you mean?"

"I don't know. Could he have gone there and not done all the praying and stuff?"

"What do you know of a man named Marston?"

"He's a lawyer."

"Has he done work for Connolly?"

"I suppose so. They knew each other."

"Well?"

"In a business sort of way."

The name Crispi drew a blank. So did Wolmer and Leahy. Browner she knew. She had an insurance policy with him. Connolly had recommended him. It turned out that Connolly paid the premiums on the policy. Her son was the beneficiary.

"Dolores?"

"Dolores? Is that a last name or what?"

Keegan hadn't thought of that. He asked Caroline Perth why she had. Because the others had been men, she supposed.

"Is it possible you had a rival?"

"A rival?"

"Yes," Keegan said patiently. "Was Connolly tiring of you? Was he thinking of replacing you perhaps? Was he starting to take out a girl named Dolores?"

"If he was I didn't know anything about it. Anyway, I don't believe it."

"Mrs. Perth." Keegan sat forward. "I'm not sure you grasp the seriousness of your position. A man has been brutally murdered. Somebody shoved an ice pick into George Connolly's chest, Mrs. Perth. Do you realize that? You heard about his death, you knew we needed information about this man when Lieutenant Horvath went to see you. But you weren't very forthcoming with him, were you? Understand this, Mrs. Perth. I don't have one good lead to go on in order to find George Connolly's murderer. So far you are as good as anything I have. I can hold you as a material witness. I could even hold you on suspicion of homicide. No, let me do the talking for a moment. I can book you and put you in a cell and feed you to the newspapers. They would love to have you. And that is just what I am going to do if you don't start leveling with me. You have been sleeping with George Connolly for months all over the map of Illinois, by your own admission. Someone hired a private investigator to follow you two around. Now one or the other of you must have had some inkling of that. I want full and informative answers to my questions. Is that clear? And let's start at the end. Where were you on Sunday night?"

His homily had turned her into an adversary, but she was scared now. Her status had changed from that of wronged woman to mistress and now to potential suspect since she had entered Keegan's office. No doubt she deeply regretted having come.

"I was home. I was home all day. We were down at the pool in the afternoon, but we never left the area of the apartment."

"Your child and yourself?"

"That's right."

"What time did you retire?"

"About midnight."

"What time did you put your child to bed?"

[125]

"At seven-thirty."

"All right. Now, is there anyone who would know that you were home during that period?"

"Yes."

"Who?"

She let out her breath like a diver at the end of the board. "George Connolly."

"He telephoned?"

"He came to the apartment that night. He was with me from eight o'clock until midnight."

18

HORVATH's delight at bringing in Findley diminished when he saw how the private investigator lived. He picked up the key and the room clerk at the desk and went up. The sound of the door opening did not waken Findley. Horvath told the clerk to beat it. A gun lay on the table beside the bed. Horvath picked it up and put it in his pocket before rousting out Findley.

The little man angrily came back to consciousness, his hand slapping around on the table beside him. He peered at Horvath. It was clear he could not see.

"What the hell is this?"

"Get dressed, Findley. We're going downtown."

"Oh, come on. Not again."

"Captain Keegan wants to see you. And he doesn't want to be kept waiting. Where are your glasses?"

Findley seemed about to deny that he used them, but that would have been ridiculous. "They're contacts. In the bathroom." Findley rubbed his whiskers. "Give me a minute."

"Not this morning, Findley. Just put on some clothes, put in your contacts, and let's go."

"I've got to shave."

"Findley, get it through your head, will you? This is a pinch. I'm running you in."

"Sure you are. You're going to hang Connolly's murder on me."

"That's right."

Findley laughed, a thin laugh that seemed squeezed from somewhere in his narrow chest. In the bathroom he blinked his contacts into place. "Where's my gun?"

"You won't need it."

"You know I have a permit."

"You're under arrest, Findley. You don't have to answer any questions. You know the drill."

"Oh, go to hell. Horvath, what is going on?"

"A lady has sworn out a complaint against you."

"I don't believe it."

But obviously he did. They left the room in silence, they went down in the elevator in silence. As they crossed the lobby, Findley moved ahead of Horvath, as if to diminish the fact that he was being hustled away by the police.

"Caroline Perth," he said in the car.

"That's right."

"She's dumber than I thought."

"Yeah. Why couldn't she be smart like you?"

But Horvath felt no triumph. He had dreamed of this day and now that it had arrived the victory was hollow. The wonder was that Findley had managed to postpone it for so long. Horvath was happy to turn Findley over to Keegan. When Findley saw Caroline Perth sitting there, he just shook his head sadly. She ignored him, or tried to. Horvath took Mrs. Perth to his office.

"Why didn't you tell me about you and Connolly?" he asked, when the questioning got to that point.

"It's not the sort of thing I'm likely to bring up, is it?"

"The man had been killed."

"All the more reason."

When she told him Connolly had been to her apartment on Sunday night, one huge hole in the events they were trying to reconstruct was filled. And now Findley really was in trouble.

And that is what Horvath pressed him on when his turn with the little detective came.

"You knew he was at her apartment Sunday night, Findley. You knew we were investigating his death. Tell me that isn't relevant?"

"Okay, okay. I admit it."

"You admit you tailed Connolly to Mrs. Perth's apartment on Sunday night?"

"What's to admit? I had him under surveillance."

"And when he left town on Saturday in a VW bus with five other men, you followed him?"

"I told you. I had him under surveillance."

"How did you manage that while he was at Assisi House?"

"You've done stake-outs, Horvath. Besides, he was

there without a car. I relaxed. I relaxed too much. Sunday night I was up the road at a bar when this guy came in who works at the house. That made me uneasy, I don't know why. So I called and asked to speak to Mr. Connolly. No one could find him."

"You telephoned Assisi House? What time was that?"

"Eight o'clock."

"Then what?"

"I drove down the road and parked. There was a car missing from the lot. The only car that had been there. So I beat it to Caroline Perth's. And there was the car."

"You were lucky."

"I know."

"What time did he leave?"

"Midnight, more or less."

"And he drove right back to Assisi House?"

Findley nodded. Horvath looked at him. Was Findley really so dumb? He was putting himself right at the scene of the murder and at approximately the time it happened. Had he done it? Horvath wished Findley had insisted on having a lawyer now, it was his right, as they had reminded him, but Findley was cocky. He could handle an interrogation. He had done plenty of them himself in his day.

"Who are you working for, Findley?"

He had already told Keegan, but it was the piece of information Findley most disliked giving. In a way, it released his client, or loosened Findley's claim on him. What had been private was now divulged, and how could Findley collect?

"Mrs. Connolly's brother."

"He hired you to collect information on George Connolly?"

"He wanted everything. He never had enough. But it was the playing around he was after. The joke is he didn't need me to find out about it. They weren't exactly furtive, Connolly and the Perth woman."

"But he might have been recognized."

"Maybe. I guess you're right."

"What's his name?"

"Gregory."

"Gregory what?'

"Just Gregory. I think it's his last name."

"Where does he live?"

"I don't know."

"Come on, Findley. What is your client's address?"

"Horvath, I don't even know what town he lives in, let alone his address."

"You didn't go to work for someone without knowing where you could get in touch with him."

"He got in touch with me."

"You sent him no reports?" There had been a portable typewriter in Findley's apartment, on the coffee table in front of the living room couch. The apartment was his office, that coffee table his desk.

"He picked them up. That's when he paid me."

Keegan came into the room, indicating to Horvath that he should continue.

"Okay," Horvath said. "You were hired by a man named Gregory, you don't know if that's his first or last name, you don't know where he lives, and he wanted reports on Connolly's playing around."

"Don't make it sound like a mystery. He's Mrs. Connolly's brother."

Keegan said, "Bad news, Findley. Mrs. Connolly doesn't have a brother."

Findley looked at him. He began a protest, then stopped. It dawned on him that either Mrs. Connolly had a brother or she didn't.

"How do you know?" he asked Keegan.

"Mrs. Connolly. So Gregory is indeed a mysterious person, Findley. In fact, he is so mysterious, I am going to assume he doesn't exist. I am going to assume that you were tailing Connolly in order to blackmail him. For money. You followed Connolly back to Assisi House the night he was murdered. You'd better get a lawyer, Findley. I'm charging you in Connolly's death."

"I didn't do it, Keegan. Honest to God I didn't."

"Then you must have seen who did."

"I didn't. I was parked on the road, the county road. I figured, now he's back, I can see if he comes out, relax. Anyway, he had to be down for the night, didn't he? He'd played hooky once, now he could get a good night's sleep."

"Tell it to a lawyer. Take him and book him, Horvath. Get him out of my sight."

19

AFTER a conference Father Placidus was bathed in honest sweat and there was a look of satisfaction, doubtless justifiable, on his face. Emerging from the chapel, he ran into Father Dowling as he was coming in from outside.

"Come have a beer," Placidus cried, taking Dowling by the elbow and steering him into the refectory. "Been outside? Glorious weather. Bit muggy but the evenings are nice. Are you feeling settled in now? Anything you need, just holler. Terrence!" he hollered. "Terrence!"

The brother slid the serving door open and looked out, aggrieved. He did not like being summoned in so peremptory a manner.

"Two beers, brother."

"Just one," Dowling corrected.

"You don't want a beer?" He lowered his voice. "Would you like a drink?"

Dowling smiled. "I don't drink, Father."

"Then have a lemonade, a sarsaparilla. Brother, what do people drink who don't drink?"

Terrence's expression suggested that hemlock might be a good drink for Placidus. Placidus was not always this garrulous and bombastic, Dowling was sure. He recognized the symptoms. When a man has been speaking for a long time, publicly speaking, certainly when he has been preaching, there is an aftermath when he must wind down, when, in a word, it is difficult to shut up. Placidus was currently undergoing this withdrawal. He splashed the beer Terrence brought him into a glass and carried it swiftly to his lips. He wiped his mouth on the back of his hand, heaving a seraphic sigh. The laborer is worthy of his hire, and indeed Placidus might have been a well-digger or gandy dancer. The beer stilled his tongue. Terrence had given Dowling a glass of lemonade, an undersweetened brew that puckered the inside of his mouth.

"The conferences going well?"

Placidus nodded.

"Do you find it difficult, preaching to just five people? Or do you just talk?"

"I preach, Father. I never tailor my content or de-

[132]

livery to the size of the congregation or to the size of the church. I preach in that chapel in exactly the same way I preach in a cathedral."

Dowling could vouch for this. He had heard Placidus's orotund voice from as far away from the house as one hundred yards. Placidus belonged to the old school, to the Fulton Sheen school, of preaching. He used his voice as a musical instrument: he whispered, he roared, he flung rhetorical questions, he demolished opponents of the truth. It was a striking image, Placidus orating in the little chapel before that indifferent audience of five. Except for Marston, of course. Marston professed to find the retreat valuable. Perhaps they all did.

From the table where he and Placidus now sat in the refectory, Dowling could see the friar's clients in the hall. Placidus called out to them that cold drinks were available, but they declined, one and all.

"There's a Coke machine in the hall." Placidus shook his head. "That stuff will rot their tubes."

"Have you been at Assisi House long, Father?"

"Better part of a year. What is the better part of a year? You may have noticed that we are not overly busy here just now. The provincial would like something done about it. We are going to have to have a lot more cooperation from our parishes than we've been getting. Why, this place should be packed, at least on weekends. It will be. I promised the provincial. I am more or less the troubleshooter in the province, Father. They keep moving me about. Never been in the same place two years. A rolling stone."

"I suppose you know everyone in the province?"

Placidus leaned forward. "That, Father Dowling, is no longer the distinction it might once have been. But I suppose the diocesan clergy has been hit as badly as we have. We're understaffed, Father. Dangerously understaffed."

"Then you must know Father Blaise."

"He's dead, you know."

"This is quite a young man. I met him right here in the chapel Sunday night."

"Blaise died in, let me see." Placidus studied the ceiling. "Nineteen forty-nine. No, nineteen-fifty. I remember, the Korean war broke out right after he died. I connect the two because he had been a chaplain in World War Two and he didn't think the war was over, not by a long shot. And he was right. Course he never lived to see it. You knew Blaise, did you?"

"No. I'm speaking of a young man, thirty, not much more. He was here at Assisi House on Sunday night. A Franciscan. He was wearing the habit. He introduced himself to me in chapel. He said his name was Blaise."

"Impossible."

"It happened, Father," Dowling said patiently.

"I mean the name. Can't be Blaise. We don't have a Blaise in the province. Haven't had since nineteen fifty. You must have got the name wrong."

"I suppose that's possible. What *was* the name of the young Franciscan who was here on Sunday?"

"Father, the only ones in the house are Cyprian, Pius, Terrence, and myself. You know Terrence. He's the young fellow we got our drinks from."

"Yes, I know Terrence."

"So you don't mean him?"

If anything, Father Dowling's memory of Blaise was more vivid than before. That the very existence of the young Franciscan should be problematic lent him a stronger claim on Dowling's mind. Of course he could not doubt that he had met Blaise. No more could he doubt that he seemed to be the only one who had. But was that the case? It was clear that none of the Franciscans knew of the fifth friar who had been in the house Sunday. Could he have been missed by the retreatants as well? Dowling decided to make inquiries. The presence in the house of an unaccounted-for man on the night of Connolly's murder was not simply a matter of idle curiosity. Phil Keegan had noted his description of Blaise, but the elusive young man did not seem to figure prominently in the investigation of Connolly's death. It was difficult to say that he should, particularly if no one else had noticed him.

"Frankly," Wolmer said to him later, "the first few days they all looked alike to me. It took me a while to tell Placidus and Cyprian apart. The little guy, okay. Pius."

"Because he's older. You would have noticed someone considerably younger than Cyprian and Placidus, wouldn't you?"

"You mean Chubby in the kitchen?"

"For example."

"That's because you only see him in the kitchen."

"You never saw a younger Franciscan in the chapel? Say, on Sunday?"

"Are they missing one?"

Dowling laughed. No point in pushing it further. He drew a blank with Browner too.

"Frankly they make me uneasy. It's different with you."

"We're all priests."

"But I'm not Catholic."

"You're not?"

Browner looked sheepish. "Does it matter? I mean, shouldn't I have come?"

Dowling assured him that the Franciscans were delighted to have him, but Browner's confidence made him uneasy. Had the ebullient insurance man been receiving communion too? And if he had, what did he think he was doing when he did? This was something he must mention to Pius. Certainly Browner would mean no disrespect, indeed he might

[135]

well think he was being courteous in doing so, but either one was in communion or one was not. Dowling knew there were now priests who would distribute the eucharist to all and sundry, regardless of belief. He also knew they were wrong to do so. He rather doubted that the Franciscans of Assisi House were of the antinomian sort.

Leahy hadn't seen Blaise either. Dowling could smell liquor on Leahy's breath. He remembered that Connolly had asked him for a drink on Sunday night when he was looking for a car. Of course that had been merely a ruse after he had gotten into the hallway in time to confront Dowling.

Marston was walking on the path that led past the stations to the lake, back and forth, erect carriage, arms swinging in a very precise way. Dowling wasn't up to Marston at the moment. And then Pius came to tell him he was wanted on the phone.

"I thought I'd put your mind at rest so you could concentrate on your retreat."

"There's been a development?"

"I've arrested a man named Findley. He's an ex-cop who set himself up as a private investigator. Connolly was mixed up with some woman and Findley found out about it. He's been gathering stuff on them, apparently with an eye to blackmail. He was out there Sunday night, followed Connolly back from the woman's house."

"Connolly left here to visit a woman?"

"Some retreat, huh?"

"Who is she?"

"His secretary."

"And why would Findley kill Connolly?"

"I'm sure he hadn't planned to. Maybe he had decided it was the time to put the bite on Connolly."

"In the middle of the night?"

"Why not? The point is, he was there. And he is a blackmailer."

"You know that for certain?"

"After Connolly was dead, he turned to the secretary. Forced himself upon her, using what he knew of her affair with Connolly. She was frightened by the thought of being involved in the investigation of his murder."

"But she must have known you'd find out about her sooner or later."

"She should have known, but she didn't. It left her defenseless against Findley. Later at least, it was death before dishonor, and she blew the whistle on him. That's how we learned about his shadowing Connolly."

"Congratulations, Phil."

"Luck." But the tone of Keegan's voice was not explained by the role luck had played. He counted on breaks in any investigation. Dowling felt there was more.

"You're satisfied it was Findley?"

"It has to be."

"Isn't it odd that he would start following somebody on his own? And why pick on Connolly?"

"Oh, he claims to have a client."

"Who?"

"Mrs. Connolly's brother. Unfortunately for him, she doesn't have a brother."

"There is a brother-in-law, Phil. From Detroit. I'm sure he's in town by now."

"He is. There is no resemblance at all between him and the description Findley gave us."

"How did he describe his client?"

"You really want to know?"

"Yes."

"It's being typed up now. Why don't I call you back when it's ready?"

Dowling thanked him and hung up. He had used the phone in the lobby, standing at the counter as he talked. Pius now put the phone away behind the counter.

"Bad news, Father?" Pius asked.

"No. Good news, I suppose. They have arrested a man for the murder of Mr. Connolly. A man named Findley."

Pius sighed. "Have you noticed the traffic on the road? All day long the cars have been going by, slowly. I had Mr. Jensen put a saw-horse out to block our road or I'm sure they'd just drive in. Sightseers. The police kept them moving while they were at work, but now we are on our own."

"Where the body is the eagles gather."

"Indeed, indeed."

Dowling went to the chapel to read his breviary. The side windows were open and the sweet smells of the Illinois August came to him. *Benedicite omnia opera Domini, Domino.* He tried to feel freed of the puzzle of Connolly's death. It was a distraction to think of it now, a temptation. He was here to pray and get close to God, not to worry about crime and punishment, at least not in the usual sense. Let the dead bury their dead. Well, he must bury George Connolly. That was his duty. He could still turn it over to Bovril, but he had promised Mrs. Connolly. He felt ensnared by events that prevented him from doing what he had come to Assisi House to do. Was he at fault because George Connolly had been murdered here, because he had come upon the body, because as pastor he had been appealed to by Mrs. Connolly? Oh, how easy it was to justify what he wanted to do by appeal to his duty and obligation as pastor of St. Hilary's. But it was more than mere curiosity and the nagging of an unsolved puzzle. He was not much more impressed by the theory that that private investigator had killed Connolly than Keegan seemed to be. The case had gone wrong from the beginning, and Keegan could be excused for seizing on the first genuine prospect he had. No doubt the investigation would continue. But where would it go from here? There was the name Dolores, there was the elusive Blaise, the flown Franciscan.

Dowling closed his book and sat back in the pew. There was something more involved here than marital infidelity and blackmail, something that took matters beyond the justice Keegan represented and into Dowling's area as priest. He liked to contrast his own interests with those of Keegan by appeal to the old contrast of mercy and justice. Where was the object of divine mercy in this situation, who was in need of a settling of accounts that transcended the judicial? Dowling closed his eyes and the image of Blaise formed upon his lids. Dolores, a printed name, and Blaise, a very substantial, quite real young man, garbed in the habit of a Franciscan, eager to identify himself to Dowling. Why? As a fellow priest, as one similarly involved in God's service? Whatever his unease with Blaise, Roger Dowling had felt with him, as he did with Bovril, a sense of solidarity that could not be extinguished by mannerisms and fads of which he disapproved. If they were priests together, then they were caught up in God's merciful concern for His creatures. Had his uneasiness with Blaise been more deep-seated than that he felt with Bovril? What had bothered him about Blaise? Savonarola? But he knew dozens of clerics with odd devotions, unlikely heroes. He could not put his finger on it.

That night Dowling went into Fox River for the wake at McGinnis Funeral Home. If there were some curious people around Assisi House, there were more at the funeral home. Dowling was let into the driveway by a police officer. From cars parked along the curb, faces peered at him. Some kids, mostly adults. Dowling had difficulty understanding that sort of ghoulishness. Inside he found a small group gathered for the rosary. It would have been considerably smaller without Leahy, Wolmer, Marston, and Browner.

"It was my idea," Marston confided. "You may have noticed that the paper makes much of the fact that George was

[139]

on a religious retreat with friends. Journalistic license, to be sure, but it seemed only fitting we should be here. And I have offered our services as pallbearers in the morning."

"To Mrs. Connolly?"

"To her brother-in-law. I believe his name is Hanrahan."

His name was Hanrahan. Thin, tall, bald, he stood in the stooped way tall people have, with his wife and Mrs. Connolly. The two women might have been twins. They were both weeping. Dowling took their hands. McGinnis, at the side of the room, gestured to Dowling.

"Did you see that crowd outside?"

Dowling said he had. McGinnis was furious.

"It's bad enough for Mrs. Connolly, but we're showing another body tonight and people are having trouble getting in to pay their respects. It's terrible."

"You should be grateful they're keeping out the sightseers."

"Perhaps. Perhaps." McGinnis wrung his hands, bringing his arms across the front of his body, causing the corner of an envelope to emerge between his lapels. "Oh. Captain Keegan left this for you."

The envelope contained, a glance told him, Xerox copies of the statements of Caroline Perth and James Findley. Dowling tucked them into a pocket. There was no point in delaying things here. He gathered the little flock of mourners and led them through the recitation of the rosary, their prayers asking for the repose of the soul of George Connolly.

The four retreatants had come into Fox River by cab but now each was in possession of his own automobile.

"Are you returning to Assisi House?"

"As per orders."

"Orders?"

"The police. I suggested to Captain Keegan that it was

a matter of supererogation on our part rather than obedience to his orders. In any case, we five are agreed that we should complete what we have begun."

"Where is Mr. Crispi?"

"He declined to come. He is indisposed. Frankly, I think he was reluctant to miss listening to the ball game. He is an avid Cub fan." The Cubs had begun an out-of-town series.

"He must be a man of profound faith."

"I don't understand."

"It was meant as a joke."

He had to explain the joke to Marston. The lawyer seemed unaware of the demands that Chicago professional teams make on the faith, hope, and, above all, charity of their fans. Dowling's explanation proved again that there is no literal translation of a joke. Marston nodded in attentive incomprehension. Dowling was happy to accept his offer of a lift back to Assisi House.

Back in his room, 211, Dowling thought that one advantage of these constant interruptions was that a return to his room at Assisi House benefited from the contrast with the hectic quotidian doings of the city. He sat by his window, listening to the night sounds, to the crickets, the faint stirrings of leaves as a breeze moved through the trees. There was a smell of rain in the air. Keegan was lucky no rain had wiped out Connolly's trail before his men got around to making a thorough study of the ground. Thoughts of the Cubs drifted into his head, prompted perhaps by the promise of bad weather.

Crispi. He was the only one of the five he had not yet asked about Blaise. If he was listening to the game, he might still be awake. Dowling went downstairs to the lobby. No one was there, but he knew that Pius had a room assignment chart behind the counter. Crispi was in 111, the room just below Dowling's own.

[141]

He knocked softly, not wanting to disturb the others. There was no answer. With his hand poised to knock again, Dowling thought better of it. His hand dropped to the knob. He turned it and pushed. The door was unlocked.

"Mr. Crispi," he called, putting his head around the door.

No light was on. The light from the hallway fell on the empty bed. Dowling stepped into the room. The light in the bathroom was on, the door open. Crispi sat in the tub. He must have fallen asleep. His head had fallen to one side, toward the open door, revealing his baldness. Better wake him up, Dowling thought. He might slide beneath the water. There was no sound of a radio.

"Mr. Crispi," Dowling said, speaking in a normal voice.

He stopped in the doorway of the bathroom, out of delicacy. Crispi had not heard him. And then Dowling saw the electric cord trailing over the edge of the tub. He stepped inside. The submerged radio was visible beneath the evaporating clouds of bubble bath. There was little doubt that Mr. Crispi was dead.

20

KEEGAN was determined that this time there would be no half-assed haphazard beginning. He wanted an account of every speck of dust in 111. He wanted a timetable on everyone, priests, brothers, retreatants.

"And me?" Dowling asked.

"I said everyone. When did you last see him?"

Dowling thought. "I'm not sure. I saw him after Placidus's afternoon conference, I know. I don't think I saw him again. It could have been an accident, Phil."

"Yes, it could have."

"But you don't think so?"

"What I think, Roger, is two down and four to go."

"Then that takes Findley off the hook."

"Not entirely. But I never quite saw him as a killer."

"Thanks for the copies of the statements."

"They're not much help."

"On the contrary. Findley's description of his client came as a great relief to me."

"How so?"

"He was working for Blaise."

"A Franciscan!"

Dowling had no answer to that and Keegan was not surprised. Much as he liked Dowling, he felt the priest had a tendency to avoid the obvious in favor of the far-fetched. That there might be a similarity between the description Findley had given of his client and the priest Dowling claimed to have seen in the chapel of Assisi House Sunday night was easy enough to grant. Findley's description could fit any number of people. The question was—or at least had been until the death of Crispi—whether Findley's description applied to any-one outside Findley's imagination. The trouble with Findley's client was the same as the trouble with Dowling's Franciscan. No one else seemed to have met either one of them. He pointed this out to Dowling.

"I think Mr. Crispi may have seen him."

Well, it was a theory and one to which Keegan's resistance was destined to decline. Six men had come together to Assisi House to make a retreat. Apparently they had never done this before, whether singly or as a group. He wanted a better answer to the question *Why?* than he had been given up until now. If Connolly had issued the invitation, then there had to be a reason why he had chosen the five he had, and a reason why he had been able to persuade them to accept. Neither the invitation nor the acceptance could be explained by friendship. Nobody claimed that. Well, no one was going to get any sleep until he had some straight answers.

"I think you're right about the others," Dowling said. "They may be in danger."

"That's what I'm going to try to impress upon them. Maybe fear will shake loose some answers."

"What are the questions?"

"The main one is: What are they doing here?"

Dowling asked, "Are you going to use Cyprian's office again?"

"No. I want them all together. The refectory, I think. Would you mind telling Horvath to round them up? I want a word with the medical examiner before they take away the body."

Watching the doors being dusted for prints, Keegan had the sinking certitude that nothing would be found to suggest this was other than a stupid accident. The door from the hall had not been forced, nothing about the attitude of the body in the tub suggested anything untoward, it was clear that the radio had been sitting on the edge of the tub. Stupid. Had it been an accident? Was he overreacting, trying to make up for the ineptitude with which Peanuts had handled Connolly's death on Monday morning? He heard the dreaded voices of newsmen in the hallway. Father Cyprian was talking to them, trying to make the point that not everyone who came to Assisi House met with a violent death. Had Crispi and Connolly come together? Yes. Of course what had occurred to Keegan would occur to anyone. Six men in a retreat house, two had died, one obviously killed, the other perhaps. Four remained. Keegan stepped into the hall. There were two of them, Mervel from *The Fox River Messenger* and Ninian, the stringer for *The Tribune*. The photographer, laden with four cameras, began snapping away at Keegan. The reporters turned from the superior of the house to the chief of detectives.

When did it happen? Was it an accident? What was the full name of the deceased? What make radio was it? What station had it been tuned to? What did Crispi do?

The questions budded and blossomed and Keegan gave them answers of a sort. The door of 111 opened and Crispi, zipped into a bag, was carried by. The reporters took little notice. The photographer recorded the grim passage. Keegan ticked off the names for Mervel: Connolly, Crispi, Wolmer, Marston, Browner, and Leahy.

"Now, what do those men have in common?" Keegan asked Mervel.

Mervel scratched the side of his nose with his pencil, waiting. "Well?"

"Look into it," Keegan suggested. "That's your story."

Ninian pushed closer. "What do they have in common, Keegan? I don't have time to play games."

"Neither do I. That's it. I've got work to do."

They would have followed him into the refectory if Horvath had not headed them off. Keegan often found what is called a free press a pain in the neck. It would be nice if he could sting Mervel into digging something up on his own for a change. If there was anything to dig up. If not, Mervel could always fall back on his imagination.

The four remaining retreatants sat together at a small square table. All they needed was a deck of cards. Marston appeared to have been chosen spokesman.

"Is Crispi dead?"

"He is. He was electrocuted in his bath. He was apparently listening to the radio while he bathed. It had been sitting on the edge of the tub. As soon as it hit the water, Crispi was done for."

"Then it was an accident?"

"Was it, Mr. Marston? It would be nice to think so. In a way. As it is, it is difficult not to see a pattern emerging. First Connolly, now Crispi."

"But Connolly was murdered," Leahy said.

"I wonder which of you is next," Keegan said.

"Are you suggesting that we leave Assisi House?" Marston wanted to know. "We have been discussing that and are inclined to think we should if Mr. Crispi's death was not accidental. If it was accidental, we think we should stay."

"I want you to stay in either case," Keegan said. "If someone is intent on getting rid of you four as well, he will have a harder time of it here than if you are dispersed to your homes."

"He's been having an easy time of it here so far," Wolmer said angrily.

"Who is?" Keegan demanded, turning on him.

"I don't know who. It's your theory, not mine."

"Well, I want a theory from the four of you, and I want it now. I don't know if you have compared stories or if you did before I talked with you on Monday, so let me give you a little summary of the composite picture as it was given to me. First, none of you claims to have been a friend of Connolly's. I'll wager none of you would admit to being a friend of Crispi's either. Second, Connolly, whom none of you really knows, asked you to come on retreat with him and you all agreed. Not only that, he picked you up on Saturday in a rented VW bus, so that you not only came here, you came in such a way that once you got here you were for all practical purposes stranded. Some of you found reasons for being here once you got here, maybe, but not a single one of you gave a plausible account of either Connolly's invitation or of your acceptance. Well, gentlemen, we are starting a new page. From now on, I want straight answers. Marston, how long have you known George Connolly?"

"Me? Why do you start with me?"

"It doesn't matter who I start with. I want you all to hear what the other tells me and if you know different to speak up. What about it, Marston?"

"By know, do you mean acquainted?"

"Let's try acquainted. How long have you been acquainted with George Connolly?"

"Well, of course I had known the name for years. He was a somewhat prominent man, the sort of man one hears of. After all, his business bore his name."

[147]

"When did you first meet him personally?"

Marston pressed his eyes with his fingers, thinking. Keegan asked Horvath to read what Marston had said on Monday.

Horvath said, "He denied knowing Connolly, but said they were acquainted. 'I think Browner introduced us, at the Athletic Club.' "

"Is that true, Browner?" Keegan asked.

"If it is, I don't remember it. It's possible. I like to bring people together."

"So you knew Connolly?"

"No better than I knew Marston."

"How well is that?"

"I never denied knowing Connolly," Leahy said plaintively. "I considered myself a friend of George's."

"How well do you know these other gentlemen, Mr. Leahy?"

"I met them on Saturday, when George picked us up."

"What precisely did George Connolly say when he asked you to spend a week at Assisi House?"

"Are you asking me?" Leahy said.

"Yes."

"Well, when he called, he said it had been a long time. I agreed. He said you never get to see the people you really want to see and he had been trying to think of a way to remedy that. He had hit on this retreat idea. Don't be scared by the word, he said. Just think of it as a chance for a group of men to step out of their rut for a few days. I asked how many days. He said maybe five, maybe a week. That sounded like a long time to me. It is a long time. I said I'd have to think about it but he said no go, he had to have my answer right away. So I said I'd come along."

"You were surprised by the invitation?"

"Sure I was surprised."

"You hadn't heard from Connolly for some time?"

"That's right. It's true, you know. You don't get to see the people you really want to. Not in the business world, you don't."

"Okay, Marston. What did Connolly say to you?"

Marston smiled frostily. "He must have composed a little speech. Those are almost exactly the words he spoke to me."

"He said how seldom he got to see you?"

"A version of it. He said that we had met, that he liked me, he wondered if he would ever get to know me well. Short of becoming my client." Marston laughed. "I thought the idea of a retreat was fascinating, but like Mr. Leahy, five days or even a week seemed excessive to me. I too asked for time to think but he said he had to make the booking immediately and he needed my answer then. Of course he apologized for seeming to put pressure on me. On an impulse, I told him to put my name down. I have not regretted it, despite the tragic occurrences."

Wolmer and Browner claimed to have had similar experiences. That of course was the risk in a common interview. They could borrow answers from one another.

"Did he say who else would be here with you?"

Marston thought he had mentioned a name or two. "He did say that he doubted I would know all the others and of course he was right."

"Are you suggesting that you five might quite easily have been five others? That, if you had refused, others would have been asked?"

"For all I know, I was asked because someone did refuse," Marston said. "I really don't see how I can answer that question. Certainly I wouldn't presume to."

Keegan signaled to Horvath and the lieutenant took

over. The results he got were not appreciably different. Keegan was convinced they were not telling him all they could, things they knew would cast light on the deaths of Connolly and Crispi. They did not look frightened, intimidated, pressured from without, so self-interest must be the explanation of their unwillingness to speak freely. But how could the self-interest of four men, four presumably different interests, converge into one?

"There has to be some connection between those four," he said to Horvath afterward.

"I wonder if Findley knows."

Keegan looked grim. "Leave Findley to me. I want you to dig into these four. Get all the warrants necessary, their businesses, their homes, everything."

"What about Findley?"

"We've got him for plenty."

"He'll get out on bail if we reduce the charge."

"You afraid he'll take off?"

"It might be the smartest thing for him to do."

"He wouldn't get far. I'm going to have a word with Roger Dowling before I go. Are the men posted?"

Assisi House was under heavy police protection and would stay that way as long as the remnants of Connolly's group remained. Dowling thought this a good idea.

"I'm tired of turning up bodies."

"What time is Connolly's funeral?"

"Ten in the morning. Does Crispi have a family?"

"None that we've traced. He lived in his motel, seldom left the bank building."

"And people think monks live a confining life. Did you ask them about Dolores?"

"Those four aren't going to talk, Roger. I assume they would have something to say if they chose to. Do you think

[150]

they're just a random group? You have fairly good knowledge of them by now."

"No, I don't. Something binds them together."

"When you figure out what it is, give me a call."

21

IT WAS a bad question to be asked late at night, the kind of question that accompanies one to bed and keeps sleep at bay. Dowling lay sleepless, the victim of his imagination.

What the retreatants had in common was this: The four survivors had conspired to kill Connolly and Crispi and their plan was working beautifully. They had destroyed their victims and contrived to make themselves appear as the next candidates for extinction. The police were guarding Assisi House, keeping imaginary assailants from getting to the four assassins. Ingenious. Keegan could scarcely expect them to confide what they had in common.

What made Connolly and Crispi targets? Each was in

business for himself, the one in goods, the other in services. Three of the survivors held jobs that could relate them to the victims: law, insurance, sales. All Keegan had to do was to discover the business link among the five and he would have the reason for the conspiracy.

And then he could figure out Wolmer's connection with the others.

On the other hand, his imagination went on, the six men had come to Assisi House because they had in common what any random sample in a city might have in common, say, an incurable disease whose prognosis was terrifying. The victims of such a disease might very well become known to one another. An idea had grown collectively on them: why should they wait for so horrible an end? They would cheat fate by ending their own lives while they were still able to do so. Perhaps group-suicide provides some needed solidarity. We live in an age when the most private things are done in groups, when secrets and discretion and reticence are looked upon as psychological flaws and social menaces. Killing oneself would appear to be the ultimate and quintessential private deed. Dowling's imagination, freed in his weariness from the check of rational habit, found it plausible that six men should enter into a suicide pact. Perhaps a mutual killing pact: the manner of death would be left to the executioner. Dowling imagined a drawing of lots to determine the order in which each must strike. The result is not divulged. The executioner may choose his victim. There is both certainty and uncertainty. Within a week or even five days all would be dead, the last by his own hand.

It was an inconvenience that so much attention had been drawn to them, but surely that was inevitable. They would have discussed how to react to police inquiries; the main thing was to mislead, to postpone, to throw off the scent. By the time it became clear what they were really up to, all would be dead.

So all Keegan had to do was get hold of the medical records of the six men.

Too complicated? Simplify, simplify. Findley and one of the retreatants conspired to get rid of Connolly. There would be no record of it, but someone here, let us say Marston, is Findley's client. A lawyer would have several dozen ways of profiting from a death if he knew of it in advance, if he could even arrange it with impunity. Findley gathers the information Marston needs and the fact that Connolly was engaged in an illicit affair with Caroline Perth is essentially irrelevant. Sunday night Findley arrives to do Connolly in, but unaccountably Connolly is gone. The woman. Findley goes back to town, finds Connolly at Caroline Perth's, trails him back to Assisi House and murders him. Of course he runs the risk of being suspected, he is suspected. That is when Marston must distract the police by adding another corpse, one for which Findley could not possibly be responsible. Meanwhile the police wasted countless hours searching for Findley's imaginary client. Findley's contretemps with Caroline Perth was not part of the original plan and he will have to assume sole responsibility for that. Nonetheless, Findley's unscheduled vulnerability because of his antics with Mrs. Perth would be a cause of grievous anxiety to Marston.

Keegan would be well advised to look out for the safety of Findley.

And so through half a dozen other possibilities: a demented Cyprian; or better, Placidus, avenging himself for the indifference of his retreatants to the consolations of religion. Waldo alleviating a lifetime of resentment by killing off what must seem to him a group of wealthy men; Crispi's death really an accident and Connolly's a suicide, Findley having been hired by Mrs. Connolly to prevent her husband from destroying himself: on Sunday night the two men struggle in the field but Connolly retains possession of the stolen ice pick, runs to the seventh station, and plunges it into his chest.

Finally Dowling felt that he would tempt sleep more effectively by getting up and sitting by the window.

He fell asleep in his chair. But in his dreams the fantastic theories continued to build. Dominant in them all was the fifth Franciscan, Blaise, seeing himself as the instrument of divine punishment as he slew the retreatants one by one. Sometimes he was the instrument of the cunning Dolores, a medium, a palmist, someone on the freaky fringe, who was using Blaise to sacrifice a group of men who had on different occasions dismissed her powers with a laugh.

Dowling awoke unrested and sore of limb. It was after four. He remembered going out at this hour on Monday. He would do it again. But first forty winks on his bed. Before his head touched the pillow he dropped into a deep and dreamless sleep.

22

FINDLEY sat at the table watching Tuttle strut about the conference room, orating to the audience that was not there. Findley was his only listener and Tuttle's manner reminded him depressingly of his own when he sought to impress prospective clients.

"I've given them one hour to have the charge reduced and bail set."

"Reduced to what?"

"That's the problem. Blackmail, rape, impersonating an officer, jaywalking, anything but murder two."

Findley said, "I still can't believe she blew the whistle on me."

"Hell hath no fury," Tuttle began, then let the quotation drift away. "It will never come to court." He sounded disappointed. "Your license is another problem."

"If I lose my license I might just as well be put away."

"Nonsense. A man of your background can move in a dozen lines of constructive work tomorrow."

"For instance?"

"Security work, lots of things." Tuttle dismissed the problem, a mere bagatelle. "Of course there's no jury at a license hearing." He seemed to see this as a disadvantage. Findley doubted that he himself would be impressed by Tuttle, but then he already knew his batting average in court. Still, he was in no position to be choosy about legal representation. Tuttle was the only lawyer who had returned his call.

Somewhat to his own surprise, Findley did not feel apprehensive about his plight. He had not killed Connolly. Even if the other body had not been found, he did not believe he could have been convicted of a crime he had not committed. He was still cop enough to believe that only the guilty are convicted. And he had his trump, even if he could play it only in the crunch. Gregory. His client had paid a large retainer without demur and had been quick to come across with expenses. Findley had hitherto thought of Gregory simply as a steady source of income. The young man had shown no haste to exploit the information on Connolly and Mrs. Perth that Findley gathered for him. Findley had come to suspect it was only a sick curiosity. It might have been jealousy, a passion for Caroline, even for Connolly, given Gregory's mannerisms, but Findley didn't think so. He had stopped being curious. His life had become an appendage to Connolly's, he had known the man like a brother, another self, though they had never met. And then, two weeks ago, Gregory had given him his surprising instructions.

Tuttle was banging for the guard. He wanted to see what Keegan was doing about his ultimatum. Tuttle tried to

convince the guard that Findley should be left in the consultation room, but that was against the rules and, listening to the
doomed exchange, Findley found that he did not mind the
thought of more time in his cell. He was on the edge of the big
time, he was convinced of that, and he did not want to act
precipitously. Tuttle lost the argument with bad grace and the
guard took Findley back to his cell. The guard seemed to
blame Findley for his lawyer's vehemence.

"Big shot," Findley explained.

"What did you pick him for?"

Findley shrugged. The door clanged behind him and
was locked. He sat on his cot, alone, oddly content. Is this
what monks feel? When Gregory had told him what he wanted
done, Findley had told him it was impossible. He knew Connolly too well to think he would agree to so whimsical a
demand.

"I know him too," Gregory had said with his saccha-
rine smile. "How are your funds holding up?"

Findley was always ready for this question with an
inflated account of his expenses, imaginatively documented,
but Gregory waived such justifications. He gave Findley
money, cash as always, an unexpected boon, that manner of
payment, given the confiscatory rate of taxation. What did
Gregory do for a living?

"We'll keep this on a professional level, Mr. Findley.
No offense meant."

"None taken," Findley said, putting the money in the
inside pocket of his suit coat where he could feel its reassuring
bulk against his chest.

Gregory had laid out what Findley was to do, precisely
and in great detail. Findley listened in disbelief. This would
mean the end of his surveillance of Connolly. Well, he
couldn't complain. He had profited enormously and all good
things must end. Gregory went on to speak of Marston,

Wolmer, Leahy, Crispi, and Browner. Connolly was to invite them all to accompany him to Assisi House. Findley looked at his client askance. Was he crazy? He could believe it. Again he said that Connolly would refuse.

"I don't think so."

"Even if he doesn't, why the hell should the others agree? As far as I know, they aren't friends of his. I don't think he has seen any of them all the time I've been watching him."

"I'm not surprised."

"I'll convey the message, but I don't promise anything."

"One more thing." And then Gregory had given him the name, the open sesame, the reason why Connolly and the others would agree.

Findley decided that he was nuts.

But Gregory hadn't been nuts. The name had done the trick. Why?

Keeping things on a professional level meant that Findley did not know who Gregory was, where he lived, what his interest in Connolly or the five others was. It hadn't seemed important, not with Gregory paying him in advance. What the hell did he care about Gregory's motives as long as his curiosity about Connolly and Caroline seemed insatiable, as long as the money kept coming in? He didn't have to bill him. He kept no records on the case. He hated records anyway, as a matter of principle. Why should he tell himself what he already knew? Besides, for tax purposes, he wanted no record of the money Gregory gave him.

So he had felt like a damned fool when Keegan and Horvath questioned him about his client. By that time he could see why Gregory had not wanted him to know who he was. And of course he had felt like a patsy. Gregory had been setting him up. Findley was the only contact with Connolly, Findley was at the scene of the crime, Findley had a client whose full name he did not know, whose address he did not know, and he could produce no record of their transactions. He had been snookered for fair and only his irrational faith that his innocence was his shield had kept him from going out of his skull. Around him in the other cells were the sounds of despair. But those bastards were guilty, they had reason to fear. Findley was innocent. He would be vindicated. Somehow.

The manner had surprised him. Another body. Jesus. He still had difficulty admitting to himself that Gregory, that nice soft-looking guy, almost a sissy, had put an ice pick into Connolly. But who else could have done it? And now another. Crispi. Electrocuted in his tub. Findley shook his head. If he was on the edge of the big time, and where else was he, given what he knew, he was also in a position of maximum danger. If Gregory had snuffed out Connolly and Crispi that easily, he would scarcely balk at disposing of Findley.

The voice of Tuttle was heard in the land. It echoed along the aisle and reverberated in the steel and wire cellblock. The guard, his face dark with anger, preceded the lawyer.

"I said an hour and I meant an hour," Tuttle crowed.

The guard unlocked the door of the cell.

Tuttle stepped forward to greet his liberated client. Now he was playing to the occupants of the other cells. Let the word go forth to the downtrodden, to the accused, to the victims of society. Victor Tuttle was the voice of the oppressed, their vindicator, the scourge of institutional injustice.

Findley allowed himself to be shepherded through the formalities. A new charge, bail set, the bondsman standing by, and then, some hours later, he was indeed free. Tuttle had a right to look pleased.

"Your car paid for?" he asked Findley, still smiling.

Findley nodded. Sure it was paid for. It was five years old.

"I'll take a lien on it then. Do you rent or own where you live?"

Findley's meager belongings were soon pledged to Tuttle against his eventual fee. It seemed a small price to pay for his freedom. He was onto something really big. To hell with his car and cruddy furniture. He parted from Tuttle on the front steps of the courthouse.

Now he meant to find out who Dolores was. Or had been.

"Keep your nose clean," Tuttle said. "I've got some thought on how to proceed in the license hearing."

But Findley would have been willing to give Tuttle a lien on his license too.

23

Louis had insisted that she come to the funeral, so Helen Marston came. She hated funerals. She hated it when Louis insisted that she do things, a way he had when it concerned something he knew she disliked intensely. Funerals. She thought they were a barbaric custom, savage. Supposedly civilized people doing a ritual dance around the body. She parked the little car. Louis had wanted to take the large car back with him to the place where he had gone to meditate. He made it sound vaguely eastern, perhaps some guru from Mother India, transcendental meditation, one of the fads she heard so much of nowadays, but it turned out to be Catholic, a Franciscan house. "Saint Francis," Louis had explained. "As in San Francisco." Funny, she had never realized that is what it meant. But then did she stop to think of the meaning of St. Louis and St. Paul? Names of cities, that's all they were. Wouldn't it be a joke if Louis got religion?

Mrs. Marston dragged on her cigarette. She had both side windows open, for ventilation, and of course she never used the ash trays in the car. Louis was such a snoop. Not that she thought he had any inkling she had not quit smoking after he announced that he was personally convinced it was a menace to health.

She had a self-serving theory that cigarettes were bad for men but not for women. She did not like to think of cancer scares or heart disease and all the rest. Honestly, if you did pay attention to the thousand natural shocks that flesh is heir to, life would lose its savor entirely. She particularly did not like to think of what could assail a woman. Breast cancer was a phrase she could not form even in the privacy of her own mind. Since puberty her large breasts had been her greatest physical asset; she knew their charm for men and their intimidating power with other women. Certainly not many women her age could dare the *décolletage* that was her trademark. A mastectomy would have been the destruction of her self. Oh, she knew about padded bras and the rest of it, but not the least delight in being built the way she was was to linger a moment between nightie and underthings in the morning, or vice versa in the evening, to catch a glimpse of herself in the mirror. She had a bit of the nudist in her, no doubt. And why not? If you've got it, flaunt it. But think of having had it and then losing it, think of cowering in the closet lest anyone, herself included, saw her naked. Helen Marston dragged deeply on her cigarette. If cancer was going to get her she would rather have it in the lungs.

Depressing thoughts. It was this damned funeral. Funerals frightened. Look at this lovely summer day, the sun shining, the lawns still asparkle with dew, birds everywhere, and she had to drag herself into that church and be reminded of death and sorrow and . . . And of the past.

It had been so long since she had thought of the Connollys. How was Lucille taking her loss? Loss seemed somehow too mild a word. After all, George had been killed, murdered. She shuddered. It might have been Louis. The thought turned up familiar images of herself as a widow. What woman hadn't imagined herself surviving her husband? You were taught to expect it. When you're younger, it has its appeal, morbid as that may sound. One thinks of other men, of travel, cruises, the shuffling off of inhibitions. But a time came, whatever a marriage was like, when all one had to look forward to was loneliness. Poor Lucille.

She finished her cigarette and tossed it into the street. She had a breath sweetener in her purse. What a hypocrite she was. Why couldn't she just tell Louis she was glad he no longer cared to smoke but she did, and if he felt he had to, he could turn her name in to the surgeon general? But she wouldn't. She could see that godawful rational expression of his, could hear the torrent of absolutely unanswerable arguments. How could someone so smart be so dumb? Naïve, not dumb. For all his shrewdness, Helen had always felt protective toward Louis, maternal. He loved her breasts.

The bell of the church was tolling mournfully as she turned the corner and came into sight of it. The hearse was drawn up to the curb; it had come from the opposite direction. She could see Louis and some other men standing on the walk. There was a stainless steel carrier on wheels between them. She watched them ease the casket from the hearse and place it on the carrier. Louis looked like a little soldier. Who were those other men? But her attention was drawn to the widow who now emerged from a car behind the hearse, supported on the arm of a man. Lucille Connolly wore a black veil that completely concealed her face. . . .

Helen stopped, wanting to hold back from the center ring in this circus of grief. There were others there on the walk in front of the church. Helen recognized no one. She felt she had come to spy on the sorrow of strangers. The pallbearers had wheeled their burden to the steps of the church and now, with the aid of the professionals, the funeral director and his men, they eased it up the stairs, slowly. Lucille and her escort followed, others falling into line behind, people who had gotten out of other cars parked behind the hearse. Would they follow the hearse to the cemetery afterward?

And suddenly, surprising herself, Helen Marston was determined to go to the cemetery later. She had never seen a body carried to the actual grave. A ghoulish unquenchable curiosity took possession of her. She had to see it done. She must watch, though the thought nearly overwhelmed her. She felt her knees actually buckle.

The service was quickly over though it seemed interminable to Helen. Would she be allowed to go to the cemetery? Perhaps the hearse just whisked the body away and the crowd dispersed. But no, she had seen funeral processions wending their way through city streets. Had they only been taking the body from the mortician's to the church? She was actually fearful now that she would be prevented from witnessing the final grisly scene, a scene her mind was already full of in unbelievable detail, a pastiche of films and novels. *The Third Man, Dr. Zhivago,* Pip in the graveyard in *Great Expectations,* the poetry of Emily Dickinson.

It was like a religious experience, the realization that

she was fascinated by death. Why, oh why, hadn't she gone to the funeral home the night before? How had she convinced herself that she despised funerals? Had she unwittingly been resisting her very destiny? More likely this was connected with her age, a post-menopausal acceptance of the ultimate deed, the final fact, earth to earth and dust to dust.

Afterward she scooted around the corner for her car, circled the block, and drew up at the end of the procession. A man came along the row of cars and again she was fearful that she would be prevented from taking part.

"Are you going to the cemetery, ma'am?" He was in his forties, had a doleful expression, but one she guessed he put off as easily as he put it on. Their eyes caught and for a moment it was as if they were trading secrets. His eyes dropped to her breasts. Until that happened she was never sure that she was seen for the woman she was.

"Do I just follow the others?"

"That's right. Turn on your headlights." He fixed a little purple pennant on the fender of the car. She was the last in line. He seemed to hesitate before returning to the front of the procession. Helen felt she had been initiated into some dark rite.

Driving along, aware of the traffic giving way to the procession, feeling a little silly coming last, not wanting to be separated from the others, she sought in vain for an expression that would seem appropriate to those they passed. But would they expect someone this far back in the procession to be grief-stricken? Her pulse was racing. How awfully exciting this was. It was childishly fun to follow the procession through red lights, the perquisite of the dead.

She could not summon a satisfactory image of George Connolly. She remembered a stout florid man, unattractive in an ordinary way, yet somehow magnetic. Powerful. A dance at the country club, early spring, the French doors had been open and she had felt particularly beautiful, a new dress, white, daring, and she had an artificial tan from the lamp Louis had given her. The Connollys. They had seen quite a bit of them at the club in those days.

But there had been a falling out. Some quarrel between George and Louis. How odd that she had forgotten. At the time, it had been serious enough. Louis tightlipped, coming to take her home. He had been talking with George Connolly, in the bar, somewhere, and she could tell he was furious. She had never learned what it was all about, Louis could be so secretive where business was concerned. That had been the end of their friendship with the Connollys. Perhaps friendship was too strong a word. Whatever it had been, it was succeeded by enmity. And then the Connollys were simply no longer mentioned.

At the cemetery, the procession crept along a winding road among the trees, among the graves, then stopped. The wheeled carrier could not be used here and the pallbearers had actually to carry the ornate casket from the road. They seemed to stagger under their burden. Poor Louis. But her eyes were drawn fatefully to their destination. There was no question now of holding back. She wanted to see everything.

She stood directly across the grave from Lucille. The black veil concealed the widow's expression. How enormous the casket looked, suspended over the grave. Helen, on tiptoes, tried to see into the grave; she could see the sheared earth that were its sides, but only a glimpse. The site itself was camouflaged. Artificial grass, seedy matting, covered what must be the piles of dirt that had been dug from the hole. A priest, lean and elegantly dressed, his solemn expression unfeigned, read in a beautiful voice some prayers.

And then it was over. Lucille was being led back to her car. The others were dispersing. Helen remained beside the casket. Weren't they going to lower it into the hole? Louis too was going back toward the road. Helen ran to catch up to him. He turned, surprised to see her.

"I only meant for you to come to the church." His voice was subdued, apologetic.

"Aren't they going to bury him?"

"What do you mean?"

She looked back at the gravesite. The casket sat there, its dull finish subduing the sun reflecting from it. Helen lowered her voice. "Don't they bury it now?"

"After we've gone."

"But why?"

Louis looked at her. She could hardly blame him, but she felt cheated.

"That's the custom. It's easier on everyone. Look." He indicated some workmen not far off. They would complete the burial.

"Could I stay?"

"You don't want to stay!"

To contradict him was to invite an argument. Take another tack, that was the way she had developed with Louis.

"Why did you have that falling out with George?" she asked. "Whatever came between you?"

"What do you mean?"

"Remember. You had an argument with him at the country club. Years ago."

He had taken her arm and she felt a painful pressure. "Be quiet." His voice was actually menacing. "Don't ever mention that again."

She stared at him. This had been a bad time to bring that up. Speak well of the dead? But Louis's anger went far beyond being a response to a social gaffe on her part. His eyes seemed to be demanding something of her, she didn't know what. She found herself nodding, agreeing. The moment passed.

He said, "Do you have your car?"

"Yes."

"I left mine at McGinnis's. They'll take me there. I'll be home day after tomorrow."

When he let go of her arm, he stepped back. Husband and wife, they looked at each other over a gap of several inches, but she had the sensation he was receding from her. Or was it the other way round? He said good-by and turned to go almost hurriedly toward one of McGinnis's limousines.

Seated in her car, defiantly smoking a cigarette, Helen Marston watched the workmen lower George Connolly into the earth. When the dull metallic top of the casket disappeared from sight, a queer sob escaped her throat. It was not a sob of sorrow.

24

DOLORES DIMARCO had committed suicide in the Rainbow Motel on Highway 20 in 1967. An overdose of sleeping pills. It was in October, she was twenty-seven. The newspaper account was surprisingly detailed, one of those flukes due to a dearth of news. Sufficient for the day is the news thereof. Each day's newspaper is roughly the same length: one way or another the pages must be filled. Dolores Dimarco had killed herself on a day when a motel suicide had little to compete with and some reporter had gathered details assiduously. The radio she must have been listening to in her last minutes was still on during the preliminary investigation. The medical examiner and the lab crew, and the newspaper reporter, had done their jobs to the jolting accompaniment of a Chicago rock station that blared forth the Top Twenty night and day.

Those were the facts. Horvath was led to them circuitously and, when he read the newspaper account, it was with some annoyance. The reporter had used the girl's death as something on which to hone his own mock-Hemingway prose. Yet Horvath did feel the solid satisfaction that comes from following an unlooked-for lead to its desired end.

He had begun with the thought that if Connolly, pushing sixty, was playing around, the chances were that this was the habit of a lifetime carried into old age like a burden he could not put down. And who would be likely to know of the women in a man's life if not the denizens of those places where such lovers congregate: bartenders, cocktail waitresses, veteran hotel and motel employees? If Dolores was a woman in Connolly's life, she was either a present or past interest. His involvement with Caroline Perth made it unlikely that Dolores figured in his present. The past, then, and Horvath banked on Connolly's death to have stirred the memories of those who would know. He thought of the city as it had been before they knocked everything down. He thought of the places where couples like Connolly and his girl might go. A lot of them were gone now, but some remained. The cocktail lounge at the Strachy Hotel, for example.

Horvath remembered it as a bustling place, a center of activity. He hadn't been there for years and one look told him that not many others had been either. A couple of matrons sat in a booth, the results of their shopping in the seats beside them, sipping fruity-looking drinks. One man at the bar, an old but not elderly man, drinking beer. The bartender, surprisingly, was young. That was a disappointment. Horvath sat at the bar, two stools from the beer drinker. The man looked vaguely familiar.

"You're Horvath, aren't you?"

"That's right." Horvath moved to a stool beside the man, accepted the offer of a beer. "Cooney," the man said. "I'm the manager here." He looked around. "Such as it is."

"What happened?"

"Someone decided to save the city. The way they did Hiroshima. If I owned this place I'd close it."

Horvath suggested that it was convenient for those who stayed in the hotel.

"Sure," Cooney said. "For both of them. If I owned the hotel I'd knock it down and build a motel. Do you know how many cars fit into our garage? Why should you know? It doesn't matter. Even downtown now a hotel has to be a motel. That means parking space on the premises. It also means fewer services. Where's Horvath's beer?"

"Make it a ginger ale," Horvath told the bartender.

"He's twenty-one," Cooney said, meaning the bartender. "I thought he might get his friends to come here. Ha. Good kid, though."

"This place had its day," Horvath said, sipping his ginger ale. Tasteless. The kid had shot it from a hose, having dialed to ginger ale. Horvath felt he was drinking from a garden sprinkler.

"You bet it did." Cooney looked over his shoulder at the lady shoppers, then leaned closer to Horvath. "One of those broads used to meet a guy here in the afternoon, a drink or two, then upstairs for a quickie before she went home to cook for her husband and the kids." Cooney's tone was disapproving but his expression was one of mellow nostalgia.

"A hotel bar has its conveniences. You knew George Connolly, didn't you?"

"Say, I read about that. An ice pick. We had ice picks behind the bar in the old days but no more. I hated those things. Ice picks and hat pins. You wouldn't remember hat pins."

"I'm surprised you do."

"Cooney never forgets."

"Connolly ever come in here?"

"You mean lately? No." Cooney's face took on a look of comprehension. "You're investigating his death?"

"I'm on it, yes."

"Got any leads?"

"We've always got leads. I'm trying to get a fuller picture of the kind of man he was."

"A Fuller Brush man. He was an asshound." Cooney had not dropped his voice and there was a stirring among the shopping bags in the booth behind them. "A real swordsman."

"But he was married." He felt he owed this remark to Lilian.

"What's that got to do with it? Some men are made that way, Horvath. I've seen it. Others aren't. The one can't judge the other. Connolly was that way."

"Lots of different girls?"

"You and I might think so, but he didn't hop around a lot. You'd see him with the same broad for quite a while. You'd think, Oh, Oh. This one is going to get him, break up his happy home and then she can sit there waiting for old George while he's in here with someone else. But then there would be another. He needed it, but he wasn't going to ruin his life for a dame. That's the way it looked to me, anyway. But what the hell do I know? I've been married to the same woman for so long we even look alike."

[170]

"You remember any of them?"

"Connolly's girls?"

Horvath nodded.

"A bartender is the soul of discretion," Cooney said. "But how often do I get a chance to speak well of the dead? Speak George Connolly's epitaph. He was a cocksman, friends. A mattress athlete without peer." Cooney's voice rose in mock rhetoric. He sipped his beer. "Sure, I remember them."

"I don't suppose you'd remember names."

"What do you mean? Of course I would. If I knew them then, I remember them now. What do I have to do all day but sit on a stool as a decoy—you look in you know the place is really open if someone's sitting at the bar—sit here and reminisce. Drives that kid crazy. What does he care about the good old days? He likes it when nobody comes in. Some job."

"Dolores," Horvath said.

"Dolores Dimarco, sure. Beautiful girl." Cooney stopped. "God, isn't that something. Connolly killed and Dolores Dimarco committed suicide. Of course that was years ago."

Horvath nodded. There was no point in showing his elation. He didn't yet know if this was cause for elation. The chances against the girl meaning anything rose because of the suicide. Connolly on retreat, thinking long thoughts, would remember the old girl friend who had killed herself. But Horvath had a hunch that negated the surface logic. For the first time he felt a door open in this case and the fact that it led back to the past didn't bother him at all.

Given the lead, he knew how to follow it. The newspaper morgue delivered up the story of how Dolores Dimarco had died. The coroner's report was factual. The file at police headquarters was thin. Suicide. George Connolly had not even been questioned. And then another penny dropped. The manager and owner of the Rainbow was Joseph Crispi.

[171]

Keegan listened intently to what Horvath had turned up so far. This was the break they had needed. Horvath was given a green light. Keegan professed to want to know about Dolores Dimarco as if she had been his own sister. He wanted to know her family, what she had done, everything about her death and the aftermath of her death. He lamented that Crispi was no longer available for questioning.

"Find out who was working at the Rainbow at the time. Is the Rainbow still operating?"

"I'll find out."

"Find out all you can about Crispi."

"Nineteen sixty-seven," Horvath said. It was a long time ago, but then Keegan already knew that. "Chances are it will take us nowhere. Cooney gave me the names of other girls, women, Connolly had affairs with."

"Forget them. For now, forget them. I know this could be a blind alley, but what other alleys do we have?"

It was a shared superstition to deny aloud what they both believed. Dolores Dimarco and her suicide were going to lead them to the killer of Connolly and Crispi. That was the intuition, the hunch, the lucky lead. Now it was a matter of routine.

"I'd like to talk to Findley about this," Horvath said. "I'll bet he knows about Dolores Dimarco."

"Go ahead. He's out on bail now. Lean on him. I hated to let the bastard go. He's got Tuttle for a lawyer."

Horvath groaned as he was meant to. Keegan hated lawyers. They were the enemy.

25

"Refresh my memory," Findley said. His feet were on the coffee table. To hell with the papers there. To hell with Horvath too. The lieutenant was off his nut if he thought he was going to frighten Findley. Some of Tuttle's bogus confidence had rubbed off on his client. He hadn't even twitched when Horvath mentioned Dolores Dimarco. It had to be the same girl, though Gregory had never mentioned the family name. Findley had been sitting here, nursing his first beer since captivity, plotting his pursuit of the identity of the Dolores whose name had had such a magic effect on Connolly. And here was this dumb Slav Horvath handing him the answer.

"She killed herself in nineteen sixty-seven. George Connolly was going with her at the time."

"I wasn't tailing Connolly in those days. In those days I was still on the force."

"Don't remind me."

"Where does she come in?"

"I think you know that, Findley."

"You flatter me. Horvath, I am putting George Connolly and all his works and pomps out of my life once and for all. I'm likely to lose my license, right? I've got to think of my next move. Connolly is still your job. Okay. I wish you luck. I hope you catch the bastard who killed him. But I've told you all I know. I never heard of Dolores Marco."

"Dimarco. Dolores Dimarco."

"Never heard of her."

The phone rang. Findley thought of asking Horvath to leave, but there was no surer way to keep the lieutenant in his apartment. The phone was on the coffee table, nesting in the debris. Findley let it ring again.

"Your phone's ringing," Horvath observed.

"So what? I can't take on another client."

"You want me to answer it?"

Findley put his feet down and plucked the phone from its cradle.

"Findley Private Investigations," he said, avoiding the look in Horvath's eye.

"This is Gregory."

Findley felt his flesh tingle. This was like the answer to a prayer, but what an answer. He couldn't talk to Gregory with Horvath in the room.

"I'm afraid not," Findley said. "I'm rather busy at the moment. I could suggest another agency."

"You can't talk? I'll call back. When?"

"No trouble at all. It would only take a minute or two."

"Very well." Gregory hung up.

Findley hung up too. "I guess he was afraid I would charge him a consultation fee."

"Busy, busy, busy," said Horvath sarcastically.

"Stay on the force, Horvath," Findley said, adopting a chastened expression. "The saddest day of my life was the day I resigned. Of course I didn't know it then."

"It had a silver lining," Horvath said.

"How do you mean?"

"From our point of view."

"Do me a favor, Horvath. Get the hell out of here."

Horvath left. Findley stood at his door, listening to Horvath go down in the elevator. He locked and chained his door. Sitting on the edge of the couch, he stared at the phone, praying for it to ring. Five minutes, five aging minutes, went by before it did.

"Okay now?" Gregory asked.

"Yeah, sure, I had someone here."

"So I gathered. And you've been in a spot of trouble too. Is everything all right now?"

"Well, I'm out on bail."

"A grueling experience."

"You ever been arrested?"

There was silence on the line. Findley could have kicked himself for asking such a stupid question.

"No, I have never been arrested. What's it like?"

"Boring. Don't ask."

"But I'm interested. Was the questioning severe?"

"Cops," Findley said disdainfully. "I know the routine. I ought to."

"What did they seem to be interested in?"

"Connolly, what else?"

"Not who you're working for?"

"Oh, sure. But what could I tell them?"

"What did you tell them?"

"Nothing. Believe me, I wished that I could."

"Just my name?"

"I didn't tell them anything."

"Good. Do you suppose you are being watched now?"

"No." But he wasn't sure, not after Gregory asked.

"I'd like to see you."

"What for?" Findley had not imagined that Gregory would want to see him.

"I must owe you money."

"Yes, you do."

"And of course I feel a measure of responsibility for your trouble with the police. I suppose there are legal fees?"

"I've got a lawyer named Tuttle."

"Is he any good?"

"He's all right."

"I'll handle his bill. Discreetly, of course. Now this is where you are to meet me. Tonight."

Findley scribbled the instructions on the back of a bill he pulled from the pile before him. The address was in Evanston. He assured Gregory that he knew Evanston, assuring himself he would be able to find his way around. He had maps. Once he had attended a Northwestern game, when Parseghian was coach. Gregory gave him the name of two streets; he would be at their intersection. Findley was to park a block west and walk. Gregory would pick him up and they would go to his apartment.

"Then I shall see you tonight at eight," Gregory concluded.

"I'll be there."

"Good."

And Gregory hung up. Findley's expression was somber. The wolf and the third little pig. That was a killer he had been talking to. He had a killer for a client. He knew that and Gregory knew he knew. Well, this time Gregory would not be up against some old man in the dark or helpless in his tub. This time he was going to meet his match and more. I must owe you money, Gregory had said. Yes, Findley thought. You owe me money, and a lot more than you think. Gregory had become the retirement pension Findley had thrown away when he quit the force. Gregory was his financial security.

The obituary of Dolores Dimarco was a bit of a disappointment. Findley had been counting on seeing the name Gregory among the survivors. But that was not her brother's name. Gregory's interest could have been that of thwarted lover, but he would have been pretty young in 1967, a lot younger than Dolores Dimarco. The motive was puzzling then, but it didn't matter. Findley had the goods on Gregory and that is what mattered.

26

PEANUTS ordered Dubonnet, a bit of a surprise to Mervel this late in the afternoon, but perfectly okay. His father and brother would have ordered double Scotches as soon as they knew the tab was Mervel's. He himself ordered a double Scotch. This would go on expenses.

"Here's to the department," Mervel said. He raised his

glass, keeping the gesture under control. This was no bar in which to fawn over sources. It always came back to haunt you, either alfresco here or with a vengeance at the Press Club roast. Peanuts held his own glass high, revealing the damp underarm of his shirt.

"Now that the six men on retreat have been tied together, the case should be wrapped up in no time," Mervel opined.

"Six men," Peanuts said. "Were there six? Let's see. There was Connolly and . . ."

He went through them all, calling the roll. He really is dumb, Mervel thought. It's not a put-on. He is really dumb. When he had been told that the members of the Piagnonni family who sat on the city council were dumb, he had been willing to bet that it was an act, a way of ingratiating themselves to the voting public. Trust me, I'm dumb. But there was no doubt about Peanuts, none at all.

"How long you been on the force, Sergeant?"

"I'm not a sergeant."

"That takes a long time, I'll bet. I never got above Pfc in the Coast Guard."

"Were you in the Coast Guard?" Peanuts was truly impressed and Mervel felt a little sheepish. This was one more thing he did not particularly want overheard. He should have taken Peanuts somewhere else, somewhere out of the way. He was sure Peanuts would have preferred a sundae.

"How long?"

"Two years." Mervel had actually been in the Marine Corps, the refuge of any number of hollow-chested scrawny specimens like himself. He had hated it and vice versa. "How soon do you think you'll wrap it up?"

"I'm in the National Guard," Peanuts said. "Communications."

"Keegan must be anxious to get this one behind him."

Peanuts wasn't following. Mervel turned the napkin

under his glass over, to find a dry side, and, with his pen, wrote the names Peanuts had laboriously recalled. Connolly. Crispi. Marston. Browner. Wolmer. Leahy.

"There. Six men go off on retreat together last Saturday. What binds them together? What connects them?"

Peanuts hunched forward. His expression was expectant. Dear God, he was waiting for the answer.

"Any ideas?" Mervel asked.

Peanuts narrowed his eyes in a facsimile of thought. After a while, he shook his head. "Tell me, Mervel."

Mervel crumpled his napkin. "I don't know." He looked grudgingly at Peanuts's untasted wine. "Have a taste."

"Keegan told me to find out from you."

"Find out what?"

"When I told him you'd asked me for a drink he said, ask Mervel what the link is between those men. Connolly, Crispi . . ."

"I know the names. You told Keegan we were going for a drink?"

"I'm to report anything that has even remotely to do with the Connolly case." Peanuts said this with closed eyes, as if he had been made to memorize it.

"And he said to ask me about those men?"

"That's right. He said that you were an investigative reporter and would know."

A worse man than Mervel would have been angry. A better man would have felt shame. What he felt was the need for another double Scotch. Peanuts said that his now-sipped Dubonnet was all the drink he needed. Mervel sent him back to headquarters.

"Take a message to Keegan," he said. "Tell him all those men are ex-Coast Guardsmen. That's the answer."

Peanuts was on his feet. "All Coast Guard," he said, with a shrewd look in his eye. "Is that true?"

"No, Peanuts. It's a lie. What they really have in

common is that they were not all in the Coast Guard together. Tell Keegan."

"Maybe I will."

Peanuts's farewell was like a playground threat. Mervel picked up a glass and drank to his own ineptitude. Shortly thereafter he was joined by Ninian.

"Keegan refers to me as an investigative reporter."

"Well, you call him a cop."

27

ROGER DOWLING walked with Father Pius out to the road and back to the house, out to the road and back to the house. It reminded him of the seminary, the evening walk in clement weather, seminarians two by two. He wondered if Pius's stroll was an old habit or an attempt to project an air of normalcy for the still numerous gawkers.

"Two murders," Pius said. "Do you know, we have never before had even a natural death in this house?"

"The human heart," Dowling said.

"Is that what it was with Mr. Crispi? His heart?"

"I was thinking of the killer."

"Placidus was told that the police are actively pursuing the theory that the killer was one of his retreat group. I can't believe that."

"Why not?"

Pius was silent for a time. They reached the road and turned, starting back to the house. "Of course you're right, Father. The human heart. I see what you mean. Human free will is an awesome thing. A creature who could not exist without the sustaining causality of God uses his freedom to defy God, to slaughter God in His image and likeness."

"I don't suppose Placidus has any ideas."

Pius was shocked. "If he had he certainly would not have said. A retreat director's relation with his retreatants is sacred, Father Dowling. Even if they do not formally confess to him. Placidus could not betray a confidence, nor would he pass on any suspicions if he had them."

Dowling did not propose to argue the solidity of the position Pius had taken. He admired the spirit of it even though it might not be sustained by the letter of canon law.

"What of yourself, Pius? We're down to four men now. Any thoughts on them?"

"Wouldn't it be slanderous to repeat them?"

Did Pius have a notion? Dowling had no desire to tamper with what was clearly a delicate conscience. "The question is not asked in a spirit of gossip, Father. If one of those men were the killer, the other three would be in grave danger. And of course we have an obligation to prevent any harm coming to them."

"I see that, of course." Pius thought, but only for a moment. "No. I just can't imagine any of those men killing."

"Can't you? I can. You mentioned sin, Father. It is a

fact. You and I know that as well as anyone. Those voices in the confessional, they belong to the people we see every day, people like those four men. I heard confessions very rarely during my first years as a priest, because of the assignment I had. I was on the archdiocesan marriage court for years. When I did begin to take weekend assignments in parishes, when I listened to the drunks and thieves and adulterers, murderers too, I felt all that was marginal, on the fringe. Religion was meant to be wholesome, pure, a communion of saints. The white linen of the altar, not the penitential purple of the confessor's stole. But it is really all for the sake of sinners, isn't it? Christ died for sinners, for prodigal sons, lost sheep, fallen women, thieves. Oh, I know one can romanticize the wicked. It is not the wicked as wicked but the wicked as repentant whom God loves. And we are all wicked, are or have been. Certainly we all could be, and so easily. Freedom is a mystery but the divine mercy is infinitely more unfathomable. I want that killer to see himself as God does. As an object of mercy."

They passed the bench where Leahy sat. He must be the source of the empty bottles. Dowling fell silent, embarrassed to have preached to the little Franciscan. But he had really been addressing himself. He felt himself to be an object of the divine mercy and the only way to deserve that was to pass it on. Not that he presumed to see himself as some historic evildoer come home. But he had been broken on his own weakness, leveled by drink, humiliated. It had been the best thing that had ever happened to him. He might have been a monsignor now, perhaps destined for further advancement. Instead, by the grace of God, he was the pastor of a fading parish in Fox River, Illinois.

"People come here to get away from the world," Pius said.

"Yes."

"It can't be done, of course. The world is anywhere.

Men join religious orders to escape the dangers of being human." Pius smiled. "Not as much as they used to, of course. Nowadays the dangers are not recognized."

They went into the building and sat on plastic-cushioned chairs in the lobby. Pius talked on and Dowling felt that he owed the old priest his ear. From vocations, Pius turned to talk of the Third Order, an affiliation with the Franciscans open to secular priests and to laymen, men still living in the world. They promised to live more seriously the Christian life and were joined in spirit to the prayers and works of Franciscan priests and nuns.

"I'm told that interest is starting up again," Pius said. "But some of our own men have come to doubt the importance of the Third Order."

Dowling himself had never joined one, but he remembered that in the seminary there had been little groups of Third Order Dominicans and Franciscans, Benedictine Oblates. Once a week they had prayed the hours of the Little Office together. The office was still part of it, Pius said. Not an obligation, of course, but a strong suggestion.

When the epiphany came, Roger Dowling sat very still. Pius had fallen silent too and, thinking the conversation over, stood.

"What of the habit, Pius? Does a member of the Third Order have the right to wear the habit?"

"Oh, no."

"It would be forbidden?"

"I don't know about that. Of course, a member of the Third Order can be buried in the habit, if he wishes. I doubt that any ever are, not any more."

"There would be records of members, wouldn't there?"

"At the provincial house, yes."

Dowling stood and took Pius by the hand. "Whom would I contact? Could we telephone?"

[183]

"Now?"

"It's a matter of some urgency, I think. I want to know if a man named Blaise is a member of the Third Order."

28

THE FOLLOWING afternoon, Keegan entered his office to see that Horvath had rounded up Marston, Wolmer, Leahy, and Browner and brought them in from Assisi House. They sat in chairs arranged in an arc before his desk. A chair for Horvath had been placed to one side, a point of triangulation from Keegan's chair and the chairs of the four men.

Keegan remained standing until Horvath had taken his chair. Roger Dowling came into the room and sat by the door. Keegan sat down and lit a cigarette.

"Could we have a window open?" Marston asked, looking with alarm at the billows of smoke Keegan exhaled.

"We're going to open a lot of windows today, Mr. Marston." Keegan indicated to Horvath that he should turn on the vent of the air conditioner. Marston looked placated.

Keegan shuffled through the papers on his desk, then tossed them aside and glared at the four men before him.

"You're a bunch of damned fools. You've had more than one chance to be frank and you've refused to do it. As a result, a lot of time and money has been expended to find out matters we should have been told by you. You have all denied being close friends with George Connolly, and in some sense that is true, at least of late. You don't like answering questions. Very well. We can start by having you listen. Horvath."

Horvath, his slab of a face like that of a recording angel, flipped open the little notebook he really did not need to refresh his memory. He began to speak.

"On October sixteen, nineteen sixty-seven, a woman named Dolores Dimarco, aged twenty-seven, committed suicide in the Rainbow Motel in this city. Death was due to an overdose of sleeping pills. There was an autopsy and a routine investigation. There was brief but considerable newspaper publicity. In a day or two the incident was forgotten. The Dimarco woman was a native of Evanston who had moved to Chicago at the age of nineteen. She had taken bookkeeping in a commercial college and on the basis of that got a job with the manager of a nightclub. She was extremely competent. Within a few years she knew the business of running a club as well as anyone. When she was twenty-five she moved to Fox River where she opened a club of her own."

Leahy said, "What has this girl to do with us?"

Keegan glared at him. "We're done with the nonsense, Leahy. Dolores Dimarco is the girl George Connolly took away from you. She was George Connolly's girl at the time she committed suicide."

"In a motel managed by Joseph Crispi," Horvath added.

"Both of whom are now dead," Marston murmured. "That does sound significant." He turned to look at Leahy. "A case of belated revenge?"

[185]

Browner and Wolmer were also looking at Leahy who tried to return their suspicion with a smile. "Do I look like the kind of man who would put an ice pick into George Connolly?"

"Did you?" Keegan asked.

"Oh, sure. And then I knocked off Crispi. How the hell could I do that? I was at the wake."

"None of us could have killed Crispi," Marston said.

Keegan chose not to dwell on that point now, but the fact was the estimate of the time of Crispi's death did not rule out these four. They might have acted before going to the wake, or even after returning.

"I wonder why Mr. Crispi didn't go to the wake," Dowling asked from his chair beside the door.

It was Leahy who answered. "He said he wasn't that big a hypocrite."

"Meaning you were," Marston said sweetly.

"I don't think he meant just me."

Keegan told Horvath to continue. Not that he did not want these four to turn on one another. But it was Marston's crust he wanted to break through.

"Some months after the death of Miss Dimarco, there was some question about an insurance policy on her life. It was in the amount of two hundred thousand dollars. The beneficiary was Louis Marston."

"Aha," cried Leahy.

"That was all explained at the time," Marston said wearily.

"Why didn't you mention this when the name Dolores arose?" Keegan demanded.

"Why in the world would I have connected that with Dolores Dimarco? Surely Dolores is not an uncommon name."

"Why did you have a policy on the life of Dolores Dimarco?"

Marston sighed. "It was a business arrangement. The

[186]

policy was in my name solely because I was surrogate for a client."

"George Connolly?"

"George Connolly."

"You said he was not a client of yours."

"*Is* not. As he is not. The question was asked in the present tense."

"Did you consider your answer responsive?"

"Certainly. I do not require instruction on the proprieties of question and response, Captain."

"The record of the insurance company's investigation certainly proves that. I don't find any mention of George Connolly there."

"Of course not. It was a privileged matter. I indicated my willingness to reveal the name of my client if any substantial reason to believe that a crime had been committed was produced. None was."

"From whom was the policy purchased?"

"I should think you already know that."

"Mr. Browner?"

Browner nodded disingenuously. "I never thought of Dolores Dimarco. Of course. I sold a policy on her life to Louis Marston. At the time I was delighted, I was really just getting established then. The company bristled at paying off but the policy was two years old and they had to. For a time, I thought that lucky sale was bad luck after all. But, as Marston said, all doubts were settled, payment was made, and that was that. I haven't thought of it for years."

"Not even when you were asked to spend a week on a religious retreat with Marston and the man who had owned the motel where the girl had died?"

"I told you I hadn't thought of it."

"Not even when the name Dolores showed up in Connolly's notebook?"

Marston said, "It's a common name."

"Surely you must have wondered why you gentlemen in particular had been asked to go to Assisi House. Did Connolly mention the name of Dolores Dimarco when he asked you to make the retreat?"

"Why would he do that?"

"Perhaps his conscience was bothering him. Perhaps he was still troubled by that half-forgotten episode. Perhaps he thought you should all make restitution of some kind."

"Restitution for what?" Marston asked coldly. "I resent your tone, Captain. I am perfectly willing to be whatever help I can be in your investigation, but I will not be badgered as if I were a suspect. Am I a suspect? Are these men suspects? If so, I think you realize this is a most irregular procedure."

"Do you mean I have failed to warn you of self-incrimination?"

"You know quite well what I mean."

"Would you like me to state that formally? Perhaps you wish to be represented by counsel?"

"Marston is our counsel," Leahy said, his voice sarcastic. "Didn't you notice how he leaped to my defense before he realized you had his number too?"

"Are we suspects, Captain?"

"What do you think, Mr. Marston? At the very least, you have withheld evidence in a murder investigation."

"Now stop right there, Captain. None of the things you have turned up is, one, suggestive of any wrongdoing in the past or, two, in any way pertinent to matters of present concern."

"Dolores Dimarco explains why six men gathered at Assisi House. Do you deny that George Connolly used her name to persuade you to make that retreat?"

"Where on earth did you get an idea like that?"

"Why is Wolmer here?" Leahy asked.

Horvath, to whom Keegan deferred, consulted his

notebook. "The Fox Tail was the club Dolores Dimarco opened when she came to Fox River. Wolmer worked for her. After her death, he became its owner. Its owner of record," Horvath added.

"Need we mention the silent partners, Mr. Marston?" Keegan asked.

Marston threw up his hands. "Am I going to be asked about my investments too? This is preposterous. I thought we were here to help you find the killer of George Connolly and Joseph Crispi."

"You're not being much help."

"That is because you persist in going down these totally irrelevant byways."

"You and George Connolly were in effect the owners of the Fox Tail club, were you not?"

"I have an interest in the place, yes. That I should not wish to flaunt the fact that I have invested in a bar is scarcely unintelligible. Such places are regarded, not wholly without reason, I grant, as somewhat less than respectable. Not that the Fox Tail is not fully respectable."

"Why did George Connolly have a policy for two hundred thousand dollars on the life of Dolores Dimarco?"

"Not for reasons of sentimentality, I can assure you. It was a purely business matter. It was a way of securing his investment in the club."

"And yours as well?"

"My name as beneficiary was totally a technical legal matter."

"But who would know that you were not the real beneficiary?"

"The parties involved."

"You mean George Connolly and Dolores Dimarco?"

"Of course."

"And Browner?"

"He was aware of it. I insisted on that. Did I not, Gerry?"

Browner seemed to be having trouble with his memory again. "I'd want to check my records, Louis. The captain makes this sound like something I wouldn't want to go off half-cocked on."

"Nonsense. Certainly you recall the letter I drafted at the time the policy was drawn up. In my office. You were there with George Connolly and Dolores Dimarco. We all signed that letter which indicated that my name was listed as beneficiary only for technical reasons."

"Why couldn't Connolly have used his own name?"

"You've already indicated why. He was having an affair with the Dimarco girl. He did not want to provide his wife with anything she could use against him."

"In a divorce suit?"

"I suppose."

"You still have a copy of this letter?"

"I have the letter, Captain."

"So George Connolly got a copy?"

"Whether or not he retained it, I do not know. Once the policy was paid off, there was no longer any reason for him to retain the letter."

"But you did?"

"I believe in keeping complete records."

Keegan sat back and studied his large hands laid flat upon his desk. "All right. Let me review what we have. Six men went off to Assisi House last Saturday in order to make a retreat. None of them was in the habit of doing this alone nor had these six done anything together over the course of the past five years at least. You all insisted on that. Indeed, none of you except Mr. Leahy indicated he had ever known George Connolly well. George Connolly's invitation lay behind the retreat. He asked and you all accepted. Why? You were driven

[190]

to Assisi House, as if to insure that you would find it difficult to leave once you were there. Six men with nothing in common agree to do an uncommon thing. Until yesterday we had to take your word on all this. It was a puzzling matter but there was no explanation. Well, now we have a link among you, and the name of the link is Dolores Dimarco. She was Connolly's mistress and she had previously been Leahy's. She took her life in a motel owned by Crispi. A policy on her life had been sold by Browner to Marston and it paid two hundred thousand dollars some months after her death, though not without reluctance on the part of the insurance company. Wolmer moves up at the Fox Tail after the death of Dolores Dimarco, apparently as owner, actually covering for Connolly and Marston."

"For Browner too," Wolmer said.

"Browner too," Keegan added. No doubt that would have emerged sooner or later, but he was grateful to Wolmer for the help. "Very well. Can you deny that Dolores Dimarco is the explanation of your being together at Assisi House?" He glared at Marston.

The little lawyer seemed amused. "You are suggesting that we convened at Assisi House with the intention of doing penance for our past real or imagined sins where Dolores Dimarco was concerned?"

"Do you have something else to suggest?"

Something had to emerge from this meeting and it was not emerging. Keegan felt he had used his ammunition to no good purpose. Horvath had cracked the thing, there was no doubt of that. Dolores Dimarco was the reason these men had gotten together. But once that was established, what did they have? Had one of them killed Crispi and Connolly? Well, why not? Dowling seemed to dismiss the possibility, and not because he thought these men incapable of murder. He had bought the missing Franciscan explanation and refused to be shaken from it. Keegan preferred to work with what he had rather than with what he did not and probably never would have. He sat forward and barked at Leahy. "Where were you the night Dolores Dimarco committed suicide?"

"What!" Leahy lurched and would have slipped from his chair if Dowling had not leaned forward to steady him.

"October sixteenth, nineteen sixty-seven."

"You expect me to tell you where I was on a particular night that long ago? You're crazy."

"It wasn't just any night. It was the night when the girl with whom you had been having an affair died."

"If you're asking me if I was affected by it, the answer is yes. I liked Dolores. Maybe I loved her, whatever that means. I was shaken by her death."

"Which was not accidental?"

"You've got the records."

"Were you questioned by the police?"

Leahy's face was grim. He nodded. "Connolly gave them my name, I suppose. What a bastard. First he steals the girl, then he tries to get me in trouble when she killed herself."

"What was the motive for suicide?"

"Damned if I know."

"Was she despondent? Was she having trouble with her business? Was it remorse, self-disgust, what?"

"I was not close to her at the time, Captain."

"You knew her better than anyone else here. What kind of girl was she?"

"She was . . ." Leahy paused. His hands were on his knees and he stared at the floor. When he spoke again it was quietly. "She was one of the most impressive women I have ever known. She was intelligent, ambitious too, but she was a good person. Attractive, kind." He looked up. "She sounds like a Girl Scout, but that isn't far off. So why did she get mixed up with me and then with Connolly? I don't know. I sometimes had the feeling that it really had nothing to do with me. It was a kind of act of defiance, a declaration of independence."

"Was she Catholic?" Dowling asked.

"Yes and no." Leahy had turned to the priest. "She'd been brought up Catholic, she talked and thought Catholic. You know. Her scale of values. But she didn't practice."

"You said she was defiant."

"It's not the right word. It was as though she were trying to prove something."

"Not a very flattering attitude in a woman," Marston said.

"No," Leahy agreed. "It wasn't. With her I was willing to overlook it."

"So you must have been disappointed when Connolly replaced you."

"Yes. But not surprised. I mean, I felt my luck had been running higher than I deserved. And I suspected that Connolly didn't mean any more to her personally than I did. The kind of importance you want to have for a woman, you didn't have for her."

"And then she died."

"She committed suicide."

"How well did you know Joe Crispi?" Keegan asked.

"I knew him."

"It was quite a step up for him, wasn't it? From the Rainbow to the Prairie Bank building?"

"He deserved it. Joe was a good man."

"Is that why you've been backing him all these years?"

"What do you mean?"

"He was blackmailing you, wasn't he? Would you like Lieutenant Horvath to read from his notes?"

"I owed Crispi money," Leahy said.

[193]

"For what?"

"It was a personal matter. There's no law against paying off a debt, is there?"

"I think that in this case the law might cover the payee."

"Think what you like."

"Did Connolly use Dolores Dimarco as a prod to get you to come to Assisi House?"

"Yes, of course. Look, Keegan, I've known all about the pieces you're laying out here. The others knew too. How could they not? But once you've put them all together, what do you really have? We don't understand what's happened, and that's God's truth. Connolly got us out there using the Dolores Dimarco matter, and then what happens? The first chance he gets, George sneaks out to see his girl and when he comes back he's killed. Imagine where that leaves us?"

"At Assisi House. Why did you all stay on there?"

"Ask Marston."

"I presume you mean as your spokesman," Marston said. "It was a group decision. We felt, Captain, that while we were in danger remaining there our danger would not decrease should we leave. There seemed to be some advantage in solidarity."

"Danger from what quarter?"

"We did not know. Of course we were not certain we really were in danger. But George Connolly had spoken like a man who was himself under instructions. If he used rather forceful means of persuading us to go on retreat, well, perhaps someone else was exerting pressure on him."

"Who?"

"That I do not know." Marston looked around. "We do not know. We gave it thought, believe me, but unless someone knows something he did not communicate to the rest of us, we could not imagine who could have put such pressure on Connolly. Crispi was doubtful there was such a person. That is why he saw no reason to accompany us to the wake. Crispi is dead. That seems to confirm the theory of an unknown assassin. We stayed on because Assisi House had become the safest place to be. Your posting of a guard after Crispi's death was enormously reassuring. I might add that I personally have found the experience of a retreat to be an eye-opener. I spoke to Father Dowling of that."

Keegan was reluctant to look at Roger Dowling. This meeting was a bust. All that remained was what Dowling, and these four men, took to be the explanation. Some unknown assassin, as Marston had called him. Keegan got to his feet and indicated that the meeting was over.

"Not unknown," Dowling objected some minutes later. "You will recall my mention of the Franciscan Blaise."

"Have you found him?"

"No. You have. In Dolores Dimarco's obituary. Her brother's name is Blaise."

"But we can't find him, Roger. The last address he had in Evanston drew a blank."

"What address was that?"

Keegan dug it out of the folder on his desk and read it. Dowling in turn produced a slip of paper, a piece of Assisi House stationery.

"This was his address when he joined the Third Order of Saint Francis."

29

FINDLEY had been waiting ten minutes when Gregory swept up to the curb in a little Fiat convertible. He leaned across the seat to open the door and as soon as Findley's seat hit the seat the car was off and running. Findley tugged the door shut.

"Where we going?"

"Home." Gregory's teeth seemed to crowd from his mouth when he smiled. "Thank you for being so prompt."

"Same to you."

The teeth again. With his gun pressing against his underarm, Findley felt safe, but not too safe. This grinning clown had killed two people that Findley knew of, and if anyone still had a theory of the criminal type, Findley invited them to look at Gregory. Bald as an egg but he looked like a choir boy. Dark slacks, snowy white shirt, skin tanned the color of honey, what jury would ever convict him?

Findley did not bother to trace the course they were

taking, though it was clearly a circuitous one. If he was playing it cool, so was Gregory. Good enough. Did the kid think
he was going to get rid of old Findley?

After Gregory parked, they walked half a block to the
building. Black onyx foyer, self-service elevator, but Gregory
headed for the stairs. He was on the second floor. No sweat.
Gregory had his key out before he reached the door. When he
had it open, he stepped aside.

"Go ahead," Findley said. He almost added, "Ladies
first."

Gregory smiled. "You distrust me? Wonderful." He
sailed into the apartment and Findley surveyed it from the
doorway. In disbelief. The place was like a church, a spooky
church: a thick smell of incense, no light admitted from outside, blackout shades at the windows. Candles flickered in
little red cups, votive lights, competing with little flame-
shaped bulbs in the wall lamps, burning ten or twenty watts.
From the ceiling, in lieu of a light fixture, hung a sort of
candelabrum in which one huge red glass candle burned. On
the far wall was an arrangement, half grotto, half altar. A
plaster statue. More votive lights.

Gregory was enjoying Findley's reaction. "You can
take the boy out of the church, but you can't take the church
out of the boy. Come in, come in. I'm not going to take up a
collection."

"What is all this?"

"Call it my private denomination. Make yourself comfortable. Shut the door, please. I'll be right back."

Findley shut the door. Gregory had disappeared, out
of the room. Findley got out his gun. This kid was a fruitcake
and no mistake. He had to be prepared for anything. Anything.

Even so he was startled when the monk entered the
room. He turned out to be Gregory in a religious habit of
some kind.

"Hey, what's this?" Findley crossed his arms over his chest and got a grip on his gun with the hand he had slipped inside his jacket.

"Fear not, it is I."

The strangeness of the room, Gregory in that robe, the poorness of the lighting, increased Findley's unease.

"Sit down, Mr. Findley. Our great work is not yet done."

"Your work," Findley corrected. "Not mine."

"I want to hear all about the police interrogation." Gregory flopped into a chair that was covered in velveteen. "All about it." His face was bright with curiosity, unfeigned. Was he looking forward to the experience himself? Well, if that is what he wanted, Findley could oblige.

"No, no," Gregory interrupted, when Findley began to describe the physical details, the routine, the interrogation room, the cell. "What did you tell them about me?"

"There wasn't anything I could tell."

"You must have told them you were in my employ."

"I had to. My license depends on my cooperating with the police in matters of . . ." He stopped. Neither of them had yet said the magic word that connected his surveillance of Connolly with his death at Assisi House.

"Murder? That is an inappropriate word in this case. I prefer execution. We are instruments of justice, Mr. Findley, neither more nor less. Is a judge a murderer? Is an executioner a murderer? Are you armed?"

The direct question caught Findley offguard. When he withdrew his hand from his jacket it held the gun. It did not give the reassurance it should have. "Yes."

"I thought as much." Gregory reached for a decanter of wine on the table beside him. His eyes remained on the gun as he removed the stopper. "Wine?"

"No."

"Oh, but you must. The gun is inadvisable, Mr. Findley. Do you think I have put you into too delicate a position? Who besides yourself has even seen me? Who else could connect me with the events at Assisi House? I'll wager that the police are even skeptical of my existence." Gregory laughed lightly and, turning, poured two glasses full of wine. He handed one to Findley. "I shall give you a better guarantee of safety than that gun."

Findley took the glass with his free hand. "What's that?"

"First there is our financial transaction."

Did no one else know about Gregory? This was a wrinkle Findley had not counted on. But the danger involved in his being the only one who knew Gregory, who could connect him with Connolly, was also his chief advantage.

"How much?" Gregory had taken a wallet from the side pocket of his robe. The white cincture flipped across the arm of his chair and lay there, white on black, asplike, ominous. Findley had always been nervous with priests and nuns. Even if Gregory was an impostor, his robe reminded Findley of stories of sin and damnation and eternal punishment. "Someone else knows, Mr. Findley."

"Who?"

Gregory giggled. "A fellow cleric." He began to pull bills from the wallet and toss them carelessly toward Findley so that they fluttered to the floor. They were bills of large denomination, fifties, hundreds. Findley's throat went dry at the sight of them. He wanted that money but even more he wanted the assurance of a steady stream, his lost pension. He sipped his wine.

"Seven hundred and fifty," Gregory said, as if he had been counting all along. "Eight hundred."

"Not enough," Findley said. He leaned forward. Gregory had to know the nature of his expectations, the extent of his demands. He had to realize he had delivered himself into Findley's hands. He had to . . .

His last clear notion was of an impossible gilded future, the past redeemed, security and indolence blessedly combined, Findley a figure of honor. The first spasm twitched his body violently. The gun flew from his hand. He tried to get to his feet, but then he was thrown back into his chair by the second spasm, more violent than the first, as if a lifetime of external opposition had coalesced into a single enemy and invaded his body, attacking him from within. He was hurled to the floor but before he hit it his longed-for future erupted in a great burst of light and then extinguished itself.

Gregory put a sandaled foot on the shoulder of his fallen guest, continuing to deal money from his wallet, the mammon of iniquity, thirty pieces of silver certificates.

30

ROGER DOWLING had not edified himself with his stubborn
insistence that he meant to remain at Assisi House and continue his retreat.

"Just for tonight, Roger," Keegan said. "Believe me,
Marie Murkin would appreciate reinforcements."

This appeal to his sense of guilt had done no good.
The situation at the rectory was, as he had occasion to learn
after the funeral of George Connolly, impossible but tolerable.
Marie would make it through the week. The prognosis on
Bovril was another matter. But Roger Dowling had set aside
this week for his annual retreat and, though everything
seemed to have conspired to prevent his making it, he would
not admit defeat. He had not sought distractions; they had
thrown themselves in his path and once he had stumbled over
them, he could not have turned away. Two bodies, a funeral,

the commotion of a police inquiry. A belief in Providence permitted contradictory interpretations of all this: God did not want him to make a retreat or God was testing his resolution to make a retreat by increasing the difficulty of doing so. The second view seemed, on balance, the saner of the two.

"You mean you want the peace and quiet?" Keegan said. "You'll have more of both in your room in Saint Hilary's rectory."

"There I'd be on call."

"Here you're constantly tripping over corpses."

"I'll watch my step."

"Roger, for the love of God. It's dangerous here. Isn't that what you've been trying to convince me of?"

"If it's safe enough for the others, it's safe enough for me."

Keegan sat down, frowned for a moment, and then explained to Dowling that the others would not be in Assisi House that night. Their rooms would be occupied, but by police. Keegan did not intend for the death count to rise, however far-fetched that possibility seemed to him.

"There you are, then," Dowling said. "How could I be safer, surrounded by police?"

Dusk came on at eight o'clock. The corridors and common rooms of Assisi House had been emptied an hour before. The substitutes for the surviving retreatants were in their assigned rooms, awaiting they knew not what. Dowling sat in the chair near his window, reading the *Summa* in the dying light, the treatise on Christ's passion. When he lifted his eyes and saw how dark it had become, he set the book aside. His gaze went along the path, from station to station of the outdoor Way of the Cross, long-distance devotion. The peace he had dreamed of seemed finally to have been granted him.

During the coming year he would celebrate both his fiftieth birthday and the twenty-fifth anniversary of his ordination to the priesthood. Twenty of those years had been spent as a canon lawyer on the archdiocesan marriage court, two decades of spiritual attrition, of the letter that killeth, of constant immersion in the failed lives of others who demanded a second chance. Were they wrong to direct their hope to a new beginning in time? They dream of happiness, of course, how could they possibly avoid that trap? It was convenient to think it a modern aberration, a secular dogma that each man had a right to the fulfillment of his dreams and wishes. Who could possibly guarantee such a demand? Certainly not man. Nor the Church. The liturgy of the nuptial Mass that had been celebrated for the couples with whom he dealt seemed to Roger Dowling a masterpiece of wisdom. How far its picture of what lay ahead was from the frothy unrealism that bombarded the bride and groom from the world around them. A society in which any marriage that survived was a rarity insisted on elevating ever higher its demands on the union of man and wife. The Church knew better. The Church spoke differently, but how many in the joyous din of their marriage day had really listened? The bride no longer simply hoped for bliss: she expected and demanded it, while the groom seemed to think he was being issued a divine sanction for unbridled and consummate sensuality. Chastity had come to mean a demand made only on priests and nuns and it was a demand that they, more products of the modern world than of their spiritual training, sometimes found too onerous.

His own first fervor as a priest had been a casualty of routine. The ease with which he could see the flaws in the lives of those whose marriages floundered deserted him when he reflected on himself as a priest. He had known ambition. He had seen his work as a stepping stone. Upward. Upward to what? Clerical ambition is easily disguised from one in its grip by platitudes of service. He had never explicitly formed in his mind the desire for ecclesiastical advancement, but of course he had realized that, as a canon lawyer with his assignment, he was a member of the fairly small pool from which the bishops of the nation are selected. The drinking that had brought him low had made nonsense of these scarcely conscious expectations. It was only when it would have been absurd for him to have them that he realized he had been fostering them all along.

By falling he had risen. That essential paradox of the faith should not have surprised him, but it did. His weakness freed him from the bonds of a more subtle weakness. His former colleagues doubtless saw his assignment to St. Hilary's in Fox River as exile, a seal on his failure, almost disgrace. He saw it as his salvation.

He stood and stretched. The thought of an early bedtime and a fresh start in the morning appealed. But first a visit to the chapel.

The corridor outside his room stretched empty to the east end of the building. The ceiling lights were on. He opened the door of the staircase and started down. It was impossible to believe that this quiet house was poised for some violent strike.

When he emerged on the first floor, in the area off which the refectory, rec room, and chapel opened, he was struck by the emptiness and brightness. Every light seemed on in the deserted house. At the end of the first-floor corridor stood a figure in Franciscan garb.

Father Pius raised his hand. Dowling returned the greeting and then realized that Pius was beckoning to him. He went down the corridor to join the little priest.

The lobby and office area behind the counter were brightly lit. "I feel like a ghost," Pius said. "Remember the Grand Silence?"

Dowling smiled. "I do indeed." In the seminary, from night prayers until after Mass the following morning, the rule of silence had been observed. Dowling remembered whispered exchanges like this one with Pius.

Pius said, "I've actually been sent to bed."

"Oh?"

"By Captain Keegan."

The door of Cyprian's office opened and the stern face of Phil Keegan looked out. "There isn't much point to this if you're going to be running around."

"But wouldn't a visitor expect to see me?" Pius asked.

"And me," Dowling said. "We're decoys."

"Please go to bed."

Pius bowed. Phil withdrew, closing the door behind him. Dowling realized that the light in the office had not been on. He said good night to Pius.

"God bless you, Father. I'll see you in the morning."

When he retraced his steps down the corridor, another door opened. Horvath. The light in this room was on. Dowling explained that he had been talking to Pius. The little Franciscan was still in view. He waved to Horvath.

"Good night, Lieutenant," Dowling said.

"Good night."

The door closed. Dowling went on. His hand was on the knob of the stairway door when he remembered why he had come down. He turned and crossed to the chapel.

He knelt in a back pew of the empty chapel. The only light was a small ceiling spot in the sanctuary that threw a puddle of light on the tabernacle. Dowling put his face in his hands. He tried to empty his mind as he adored his sacramental Lord.

How much later he did not know, his attention was brought back to the environing chapel. He kept his face in his hands. He had the memory of a sound, but he was not sure. The presence of someone else was strong upon his senses. And then, unmistakably, there was a sound. Still on his knees,

Dowling turned. In the confessional box behind him, looking out over the little Dutch door of the central section, the curtain pushed aside, was Blaise.

For a moment they stared at each other. The smile on the young man's face was as Dowling had remembered it. The face seemed pale in the shadow of the confessional, disembodied. Then the half door swung open and Blaise stepped out, clad as before in a Franciscan habit.

"You've come back," Dowling said. He got up from his knees and stepped into the aisle to face the young man.

"I seem to be expected."

"Oh, I wasn't sure you would return."

"I meant the others."

Dowling felt no impulse to mislead Blaise. Anyone who had been able to get into the chapel unseen would surely have discovered that the house was full of police.

"Would you care to continue your devotions outside, Father Dowling? We could make the stations of the cross together."

"I doubt that we could leave without being seen."

"Let's find out, shall we?"

Blaise put his hands to his shoulders and flipped the cowl over his head, becoming with the gesture an anonymous religious. He gestured to Dowling to go to the chapel door. Before Dowling could push it open, Blaise was beside him. His voice was calm yet urgent.

"We shall go directly through the refectory to the kitchen and then outside. Do you understand?"

Dowling nodded. He felt in the power of a maniac.

Blaise pushed the door open, his hand closed on Dowling's arm, and they were off. What had seemed the vast expanse of the hall had diminished. They were into the refectory and moving among the tables before the chapel door closed quietly on its compressed air lock. Blaise opened the kitchen door and guided Dowling through it. Dowling did not resist. He felt he was removing a danger to Keegan's men and leading Blaise from a menace he imperfectly understood. And then he noticed what Blaise had in his free hand.

"Not a gun, Father Blaise."

"It's not mine."

"Hardly the thing for a cleric to be carrying."

Blaise beamed. "But you forget the Crusades, Father Dowling. You forget the popes who led their troops into battle."

"Is your cause as just?"

"It is the epitome of justice," Blaise said, and Dowling saw that he was completely serious despite the porcelain smile.

The door that led outdoors from the kitchen was heavy. After they had stepped into the night, Blaise eased the door shut with the hand that held the gun. It clicked, locked, and they turned to the path.

Someone stepped from the shadows at the corner of the building.

"Who's there?"

It was one of Keegan's men. Dowling managed to get a grip on Blaise's hand. "Father Dowling," he said to the shadowy form. "Father Pius and I are going to say the stations."

"What do you mean?"

Blaise was struggling against Dowling's grip, trying not to make a conspicuous fuss. Dowling explained to the officer that they meant to say some prayers along the path to the lake.

"No one is supposed to be outside."

"I know. I just spoke to Captain Keegan."

Dowling took advantage of the policeman's hesitation to start along the path. "It's all right, officer."

Now it was he who slowed Blaise's pace. He stopped at the first station. "Jesus is condemned to death," he said aloud.

The two of them stood there a moment, heads bowed, before moving to the next station.

"See what he's doing," Blaise whispered. His tone was nervous.

Dowling looked. There was no sign of the policeman. He told Blaise.

"Let's go."

"Where are we going?"

"To the lake."

"Is that the way you came?"

"It is the way we are going."

Again he slowed Blaise's pace. He had let go of the young man's wrist at the first station. "If he is watching us, he'll wonder what the hurry is."

"He doesn't know what the stations are."

"Perhaps. But we do." Dowling stopped. "Jesus falls the second time," he said. He didn't know what station he had stopped at but it was too dark to matter. "Was there some significance in Connolly's dying here?"

"You thought of that?"

"Of course."

Dowling sensed that Blaise was smiling again. "The second time only in the sense of many times. Christ didn't fall enough to keep pace with George Connolly."

"Not his first fall?"

"Certainly not the first."

"That would have been with Dolores, I suppose."

There was silence. "Do they know that too?"

"You didn't expect the connection to go undiscovered, surely." He paused. "Unappreciated."

"I didn't mean for things to remain unfinished. But it is out of my hands now."

"All of them were to die?"

"Yes."

"You are a stern judge. And a loyal brother."

"If he hadn't continued, he would have been spared. They all would have been spared. I promised that and I would have kept my promise. But of course there was another woman."

"Another Dolores."

"Where is my sister Dolores now, Father?"

"I wouldn't presume to judge."

"It isn't you or I who judge. A suicide dies in despair, the sin against the Holy Ghost. She is in hell." His voice was hollow in the night air and the dark vault above them seemed to encompass a lost world, eternity and its modes, but in Blaise's voice they were closer than the shadowy cross above the station beside them.

"We can never know what passes between a soul and God at the moment of death, Blaise."

"I tried to believe that. I did. It's no use. She is damned."

"Don't say that."

"Damned, and her betrayers live on unpunished."

"And you brought them here to exact punishment."

"But mercifully. You must have guessed that. I gave them the chance she did not have, the chance of repentance. Remember Hamlet and his stepfather? He refused to kill a man at prayer, fearing he would send his soul to heaven. The justice I exact is of this world, Father Dowling. I had no wish to have their damnation on my conscience. They had the chance of repentance before they were to die."

"George Connolly?"

"I could not guarantee they would use the chance. Imagine running away from here to that woman. I had meant to save him until last."

"It was risky for you to come here Sunday night."

"Why? None of them knows me, none has ever seen

me. And I wanted to see my players in the setting I had prepared for them. The whole significance of their lives was reduced to a brief stay here. How would they decide their eternal condition? I had increased the odds that their minds would turn to God and ask forgiveness."

"As you must now, Blaise."

"I am merely an instrument."

"No man can be merely an instrument. We are not arrows or clubs. Or knives. Give me the gun, Blaise."

"My name in religion is Gregory."

"As a member of the Third Order?"

"Yes."

"Have you ever considered the priesthood?"

A disdainful snort came from the young man. "I was judged unfit for holy orders, Father Dowling. My single ambition in life was to become a priest. Ever since Dolores died, died in so horrible a way and with such a crushing effect on my parents, I determined to give my life to God, as recompense. To buy her back from wherever she had plunged herself when she took all those sleeping pills."

"God is mercy, Blaise."

"God is justice!"

Suddenly Blaise wheeled. Dowling had heard it too, sounds in the field between them and the parking lot. There were other sounds too, from both directions on the path, from the house, from the lake. Roger Dowling grabbed for the hand that held the gun, but Blaise twisted free and started to run, dashing at an angle across the field. He had not gone six feet before he fell to earth with an audible thud. His falling cry brought the police to him. Another cry, muffled, silence.

"Roger! Roger Dowling, are you all right?"

"I'm all right."

Dowling moved toward Keegan's voice, toward the flashlight that had been turned on. Horvath knelt in its light, his knee pressed down on Blaise's back.

"He has a gun," Dowling said.

"He dropped it," Keegan said, bringing the weapon into the light of the flash.

"That was lucky."

"He fell."

But the fact is that Blaise had tripped. The inauthentic Franciscan had in his haste caught his foot in the skirts of his robe. Blaise would have been wiser to have remained defrocked.

31

"TUTTLE will defend him," Keegan said. It was a week later. He sat with Roger Dowling in the study of St. Hilary's rectory where they were watching a desultory out-of-town performance of the Cubs on television.

"Is Tuttle any good?"

"No, but it doesn't matter. He'll plead him insane and win in a walk."

"He's not insane, you know."

Keegan chose not to argue about that. The main thing was to get people like Blaise Dimarco off the streets. Whether this meant prison or a mental institution was a fine point.

"To tell Blaise he wasn't responsible for what he did might very well drive him around the bend, Phil. The verdict would be self-fulfilling."

"Lawyers love insanity. I think Tuttle would have used it in Findley's license hearing."

"Poor Findley."

The private detective had been washed ashore near the campus church of Loyola University on the north shore. Tuttle was now in search of the ex-Mrs. Findley with an eye to bringing suit against the Fox River Police Department. Keegan understood that the charge would be that Findley was used as bait to tempt Blaise Dimarco into revealing himself.

"Perhaps I should sue too," Dowling mused.

"I did everything but remove you bodily from Assisi House."

Marie Murkin came in with a bowl of popcorn and a replacement for Keegan's beer.

"It's good to have things back to normal around here," she said.

"Keep an eye out for a letter from the chancery office, Marie."

"I'm not likely to miss that, am I, Father?"

"This is important. There's some chance that, if we hurry, we can get young Bovril assigned here permanently."

Marie's face fell in shock. Her hand went out to a bookcase for support.

Keegan said, "People are still talking of the spiritual uplift they felt when he released those balloons in the middle of Mass."

"He isn't coming here, is he, Father?"

The priest made a reassuring gesture.

"Over my dead body, Marie," Roger Dowling said.

3

McInerny,Ralph
    The seventh station. New
York,Vanguard,1977.
                        $7.95.1277